P9-DHT-262

"SLOCUM! CAN YOU HEAR ME?"

"Sure. What's wrong?"

"A couple of that damn FXT bunch are running the hell out of some of my three-year-old steers. It won't take me long to settle with them."

He drew up the dun and reached for his Colt, only to realize there was nothing in his holster. He lowered his gaze, embarrassed that he could neither help her nor even defend himself. They'd taken the Colt before the beating and pistol-whipping.

"Go ahead," he said, and raised his fist in a show of strength.

"Good," she said, and lashed her pony around the junipers. In a second, she was gone.

He booted the dun around the juniper cover to see what he could of the girl and her actions. He saw her gun barrel smoke, the sound of the percussion barely coming on the wind as she continued after two riders. After her shot, the rustlers decided to turn off from the group of cattle, and raced to the east to escape her fury.

Slocum tried to shake the feeling of being drained away. No use. He shucked his toes out of the stirrups, slumped over the saddle horn to stop the inevitable fall, and tried to ease himself down. His legs crumpled beneath him.

The world went black.

DON'T MISS THESE
ALL-ACTION WESTERN SERIES
FROM THE BERKLEY PUBLISHING GROUP

THE GUNSMITH by J. R. Roberts
  Clint Adams was a legend among lawmen, outlaws, and ladies.
  They called him . . . the Gunsmith.

LONGARM by Tabor Evans
  The popular long-running series about U.S. Deputy Marshal
  Long—his life, his loves, his fight for justice.

SLOCUM by Jake Logan
  Today's longest-running action Western. John Slocum rides a
  deadly trail of hot blood and cold steel.

JAKE LOGAN

SLOCUM AND THE POWDER RIVER GAMBLE

JOVE BOOKS, NEW YORK

If you purchased this book without a cover, you should be aware that this book is stolen property. It was reported as "unsold and destroyed" to the publisher, and neither the author nor the publisher has received any payment for this "stripped book."

SLOCUM AND THE POWDER RIVER GAMBLE

A Jove Book / published by arrangement with
the author

PRINTING HISTORY
Jove edition / May 1997

All rights reserved.
Copyright © 1997 by Jove Publications, Inc.
This book may not be reproduced in whole
or in part, by mimeograph or any other means,
without permission. For information address:
The Berkley Publishing Group, 200 Madison Avenue,
New York, New York 10016.

The Putnam Berkley World Wide Web site address is
http://www.berkley.com

ISBN: 0-515-12070-7

A JOVE BOOK®
Jove Books are published by The Berkley Publishing Group,
200 Madison Avenue, New York, New York 10016.
JOVE and the "J" design are trademarks
belonging to Jove Publications, Inc.

PRINTED IN THE UNITED STATES OF AMERICA

10 9 8 7 6 5 4 3 2 1

SLOCUM AND THE
POWDER RIVER GAMBLE

1

May 10, 1885

"You damn Texas trash!" Traver McEntosh swore, and drove his boot toe into Slocum's ribs. The pain from the kick was no worse than Slocum's pounding head, and the rest of his battered body, as he lay facedown in the dirt beside the corral.

"You better know what's good for you, mon, and ride clear of this country," McEntosh said. "Or you'll be getting worse than this."

Somewhere in Slocum's aching brain, he held an image, a picture of a young woman in a black divided riding-skirt. Calfskin boots to match. She was short, less than five feet tall, and wore a formfitting waistcoat and a black flat-crowned hat to match. Her lips were thin and set tight to match her hard blue eyes—no, they were gray ones that had glared full of hatred at him the entire time her ranch hands had held and battered him. Imagene Furston, that was her name, the owner of the FXT Ranch. He could still picture her thin brows, her dark hair tight in a bun behind her head. He guessed her age as mid-twenties. All business, she even wore a small-caliber six-gun holstered on her slender hips in a fancy hand-tooled holster. She looked capable enough to use it if necessary, and what the lady considered necessary was to run anyone out of Wyoming who stood in her way. Slocum knew full well that somehow he fit that category.

He could hear them mounting up, her husky voice ordering them back to the ranch and complimenting them on a job well done. Slocum did not dare move. He didn't want to wiggle a muscle for fear of more pain than he had. Also, he'd had enough fists and boots drive into his body to last for a lifetime. There would be plenty of time to discover what part of his frame remained intact when the FXT outfit was gone.

"We won't be seeing the likes of that saddle bum around here much longer," she said loud enough that he heard her. "He surely got the message to ride on."

"Aye, but you can't tell about that rebel trash," McEntosh said. "Sometimes killing them is the only way to rid yourself of them, mum."

"This should be enough. We better get back to work—we've got a ranch to run," she said.

"Aye. Sorenson, you and McElvain ride up the creek and be certain there aren't any more of them squatters' livestock using our water. Find any, you drive them far enough away they can't find their way back."

Slocum couldn't hear the rest of their conversation, only the fading drum of their hoofbeats as they galloped away. Then he passed out. He came around once or twice. But each time, his mind saved him the suffering and sent him back into unconsciousness.

"Mister, are you alive?"

Someone was talking to him. He couldn't open his swollen eyes or shake the curtain over his mental processes, but someone with a pleasant voice was asking him questions. The voice of a female that he desperately wanted to see in person.

"Yeah," he finally managed, shocked by the weakness in his choked reply.

"What happened, a bronc stomp you?" The concern in her voice sounded immediate, as if she shared his suffering and wanted to alleviate part of it.

He wanted to see her. Desperate to escape his helplessness, he blinked his battered eyelids and with some effort raised his sore face from the gritty ground. There was no turning on his side; pain racked his body when he tried. Moving his head at all was enough to force him to grit his teeth.

From the new position, he could see her chaps and dusty boots. But he was forced to quickly shut his eyes as a swirl of cool wind threatened to fill them with dirt and debris. Who was she?

"Wasn't a bronc done this, was it?"

"No."

"Is that your horse out there?"

He managed to nod his head. The dun wouldn't run far; he was trained to be ground-tied. Good stout horse. Slocum would have hated for anything to happen to Dunny. His bedroll, slicker, and rifle had been on the saddle before the altercation began—almost all of his net worth, in fact.

"He's right over there," the woman said, rising to her feet. "I'll get him and then we'll see about getting you up."

"Sure," he managed, closing his eyes at the lightning-like sharpness inside his back and chest.

"I know that can't be too comfortable, lying there like that, but there ain't much else I can do."

"Get him," he said to ease her conscience.

She left him in a clatter of her high-heel boots. He fought to get on his elbows, then clamped his molars hard shut and began with great effort to draw his knees up under himself. The strain caused beads of perspiration to pop out on his forehead. Out of breath, he rested with his legs drawn up beneath him. Elbows at his side to keep the sharp lances in his chest from becoming unbearable, he finally rose to kneel upright.

He could see her returning with Dunny in tow. Thank God, the horse was still there. Slocum's head swarmed and his vision blurred, then cleared, only to turn fuzzy again as he fought to stay up straight in the kneeling position. The wind tossed his long black hair in his face, but he couldn't reach up to push it back without hurting. Damn, those no-goods had used him for a punching bag.

"Well, you're halfway there," she said, beaming at his progress. It was the warmest smile he had seen since arriving in the territory. He guessed her to be in her twenties. She had squared shoulders for a girl, with a tomboy way of walking, and was dressed in men's waist overalls under the chaps and a faded blue canvas jumper. Her once-white hat was weather-stained, the brim curled up in the sides from reaching up and clamping it down in the wind. Her light brown hair was bobbed off short, and the wind tossed it some at her jacket collar as she stood before him.

"My name's Jenny Van Doren. They call me Jen for short."

"Slocum's mine, nice to meet you, Jen," he said, wondering which of his legs to try first, the right or the left one.

"You passing through, I guess?"

"Looking for a friend, got mix up with a Scotsman's outfit," he said, still undecided about how he would ever stand. "I guess I made some folks mad."

"McEntosh? You met the FXT bunch, huh?" Her brown eyes met his, and then she shook her head in pity.

"They got a horse brand rafter F?"

"That's them, all right. Here, I'll help you stand up."

He had seen the rafter F on their mounts' shoulders. She stepped in and assisted him. Strong enough with her hands under his left elbow, she lifted him to his feet with little effort, and then steadied him on his boots.

"You going to be able to stand up?" she asked, concerned.

"I hope so. I've got to ask a big favor. Get me over to that corral and I'll lean on it." His bladder felt close to bursting. He was unsure how to tell her about his most pressing problem, and he needed to get someplace where he could brace himself to ever accomplish the task.

"Sure thing. We can get you there, but you certainly are wobbly. That bunch of hers welcomed you to the basin, huh?"

"Yeah, she was with them," he said, taking short, shuffling steps under her support. All the moving proved was that he hurt in more places than he had even imagined.

Out of breath, he used his own shoulder for support against the sun-grayed post beside the panel made of head-high stacked rails.

"I need to ask you for a few minutes' privacy," he finally managed to get out.

"Sure," she said, as if she knew his purpose and wasn't bothered by the functions of a man and his body. "You take your time and call me when you're through."

He closed his eyes. For a long moment, he breathed in the cool air, pungent with sharp sage and a cedar smell. With his back to her, determined to end his suffering, he fumbled with the buttons on his fly, and soon the absolute relief from waiting too long arched in a stream and ran down the rails in a waterfall. He shut his eyes and savored the moment, wondering how he would ever manage to get in the saddle in his shape. His task finally completed, pants buttoned, he turned with his back to the rails to brace himself and tried to locate her.

Beyond the pens, she was on her haunches using a brushy juniper to keep out of the wind and in the sunshine. Both horses stood hipshot close by. Hers was a blood bay; she certainly rode good horseflesh.

"Guess I'll try riding," he said.

"You up to it?" she asked, rising and hurrying over to help him. He noted her rocking gait. She was hitting the balls of her feet as she came. Most women stepped on their heels first, but she gave the impression she was no stranger to stepping out either.

"I better be up to it," he said.

"There's a shack up this creek, you can use it till you get better. I'll get you there, then I'll ride over home and get some supplies."

"It belong to the FXT?"

"No. They don't own the whole gawdamn territory. In fact, most of this land up here is public lands, despite what they might tell folks."

"They're pushing cattle off this creek—" Coughing broke up his words, and if she hadn't been supporting him, he would have gone down.

"Sorry," he barely got out. They stood for a long while until he recovered his breath. Then they continued for the horses.

"They push any of our cattle out of the country, they might get a big surprise," she said.

He paused at the side of the dun. He hoped they didn't run into the FXT boys chousing stock, because he doubted he could do much to help her.

With effort, he checked the cinch. His head swirled and grew lighter. Then, with his elbows clamped to his side, he drove his left boot in the stirrup. With both her hands she boosted his butt up, and he planted himself in the saddle, checking Dunny up sharply.

"Whew," she said, and then ran for her bay.

"You sure treat a stranger nice," he said.

"Anyone runs up against the FXT like you did needs some help, Slocum. That what they call you all the time?"

"My mother called me John, but Slocum's the handle I go by."

"Don't fall off that horse. You're way too big for me to pick up."

"I'll try not to." He nodded for her to lead the way, and nudged the dun after her.

"Who are you looking for?" she asked without turning as she moved up the narrow wagon tracks that headed for the rising Bighorn Mountains.

"Nat Champion."

"They don't like him either." She turned and smiled, then shook her head in disapproval.

"I stopped off at that little town's saloon and asked about his whereabouts. This buster in the bar gave me directions to these corrals. I left there, they must have tracked me up here, and we had it out. Nat does live up here, doesn't he?"

"Yes, but closer to Buffalo. I'll send him word that you're here." She held up his hat, and slapped it hard on his head when he bent over. Never mind that, it needed to be reset. He hadn't lost anything but the Colt .44 they took from his holster. There was a spare in his saddlebags, when he was ready for it.

He heard her say something about knowing Nat very well. He realized that the ranny in the saloon had give him a bum steer to the corrals. Lightheaded, he used the saddlehorn to steady himself going downhill on the path. Slocum knew Nat from their trail-driving days back in Texas, and when the letter had finally found him in

Tombstone, Arizona Territory, it was over three months old.

> *Dear Slocum*
>
> *I know that it has been years since we drove cattle to Wichita, but I am in Wyoming now with a little place of my own. Guess it will always be the same old story, the big outfits against the little guys. I managed to get a brand registered up here and I'm running some stock. You ever get up in this country, the latchstring is out. To tell the truth, I think we may have a real case of push and shove up here this year. Lots of big-money outfits wanting to hog up everything, grass and water. You know me, I just want to make a bean and bacon living, a string of good horses and some cow stock of my own. Be good to see you, but I have to warn you if you do come, you might be sticking your old head in a hornet's nest, partner.*
>
> > *Your pal*
> > *Nat Champion*
> > *General Delivery*
> > *Buffalo, Wyoming Territory*

One thing was certain, Nat had not exaggerated about the hornet's nest.

It took all Slocum's efforts not to pass out as the dun splashed across a shin-deep creek and out the other side. He felt the blood rush from his face, and he gripped the horn tight with both hands. The action of the pony climbing up the far bank rocked him from side to side. Dazed, his vision fuzzy, he focused all his mental faculties on staying awake and not falling off the horse. It was no easy job when he was repeatedly going in and out of consciousness.

Despite the cool breeze on his face, rivers of perspiration ran down his brow and flooded his eyes. Ordinarily, he would have remove his hat and wiped his sweaty brow on the sleeve of his jumper. In this case, he simply endured the discomfort and hung on for his life.

The foreman's name was McEntosh. He wouldn't forget that Scotchman and his brogue. Then there was a long-faced one they called Sorenson, and a runt named McElvain. The other two were just punchers. One wore a blue silk scarf Slocum would recognize on sight, and the other had a red mustache as long as a twenty-year-old-longhorn hat rack. And then there was the woman herself. Tight lips and gray eyes. He wouldn't forget her for a lifetime.

"Slocum! Slocum! Can you hear me?" Jenny demanded in his face.

"Sure. What's wrong?"

"Can you sit that horse of yours for a few minutes?"

"Sure, what's wrong?"

"A couple of that damn FXT bunch are running the hell out of some of my three-year-old steers. It won't take me long to settle with them."

He drew up the dun and reached for his Colt, only to realize there was nothing in his holster. He lowered his gaze, embarrassed that he could neither help her nor even defend himself. They'd taken the Colt before the beating and pistol-whipping began.

"Go ahead," he said, and raised his fist in a show of strength.

"Good," she said, and lashed her pony around the junipers. In a second she was gone, and he had to check the dun to keep him still. He figured she needed help against those FXT punchers. His fingers reached for the flap on his saddlebags, and the effort to unbuckle it caused deep pangs in his chest. Broken ribs—he knew the pain. His breath caught in his throat as his hand went deeper. Finally, he grasped the cold steel of the barrel and lifted the revolver up into his lap.

There was no way to holster the Colt. He shoved it in his waistband and booted the dun around the juniper cover to see what he could of the girl and her actions. She was racing the bay across the flat. He saw her gun barrel smoke, the sound of the percussion barely coming on the wind as she continued after two riders. After her shot, the rustlers decided to turn off from the group of cattle, and raced to the east to escape her fury. Obviously satisfied with the result, she sat the bay down hard. Slocum tried to shake the feeling of being drained away. No use. He shucked his toes out of the stirrups, slumped over the saddle horn to stop the inevitable fall, and tried to ease himself down. His legs crumpled beneath him. The world went black.

2

The hiss of the two lodgepoles being dragged on the ground behind a horse awoke him. The travois that carried him rolled him from side to side on the groundsheet stretched between the poles when it struck a rock or hump on either side. Under the blanket, he awoke and wished for a smoother ride as he hugged himself to help stop the pain. Unable to see, he panicked at the discovery he was blind. Despite his best efforts to open his eye lids wide, he only could see through slits. His eyes had finished swelling shut for all intents and purposes. But he could hear Jenny singing some drover song.

"We drove them down the trail, just me and Todd,
Bound for old Cheyenne with a grin and a big old nod.
Move along, fat steers, don't you dally on the trail,

'Cause we have date with old Miss Ann and her
  sister Gail.
Old sorrel, keep your head up and hold it high.
We ain't got time for your bucking in the sweet
  by and by,
'Cause we're going to the south and stockyards
  we're bound.
In a few days, we'll comb our hair and put our
  money down.
Tie yi, tie yi, old pony, don't you stumble.
We ain't got time for your clumsy tumbles,
'Cause if we don't get to town by dawn,
Why, sure enough, all them pretty gals will be
  gone.''

Despite his suffering, Slocum had to grin as he listened to her clear voice singing words to a song that
he'd never heard before. After a thousand nights in the
saddle under the stars riding herd, he thought he'd heard
every old tune and rendition thought up by night herders
to let the sleeping cattle know that they were out there
riding around them.

"Hey, you're coming around," Jen said, looking
down at him as she rode alongside.

"Yes," he agreed.

"Your face sure is swollen up like you been bee-stung
all over it, but I reckon a sting would only be the half
that painful."

He agreed with a nod.

"I promise you that we haven't got but a few more
miles left to get to that shack. You making it on that
trap?"

"Yes," he grunted between sharp breaths. "Don't
stop for me."

"I scattered them two birds that were driving the fat
off my steers, and when I come back, you were out on

the ground. But I guess you recall parts of it,'' she said, riding close beside him.

"Sorry I'm so much trouble."

"No need. Any friend of Nat Champion is a friend of mine. Kinda strange, though, I'd sort of expected you might have joined Furston's outfit. She pays double wages to gunmen."

He shook his head. "No need for that. I don't hire my guns out."

"Damn shame. I was going to offer you a job when you got well enough."

"What do you need a gunfighter for?"

"I guess to match hers, but she and the others already got a half dozen on their payroll."

He tried to not show the hurt when the pole dropped off a tall obstacle and gave him a good toss in the travois. He'd be grateful to reach that shack of hers.

"That isn't the answer anyway," he said softly to warn her.

"I'm sorry, Slocum, but we've tried to be peaceful. These big outfits have pushed us to the point where we won't take any more."

"You'll go to lots of funerals if it gets that bad." He didn't want to think about the county wars he'd seen in Texas or the ones in Kansas. One such altercation in Ft. Scott had put him on the run for over a decade with every fish-eyed bounty hunter scanning a tattered poster for the thousand-dollar reward. Worse than that were the good men planted in cemeteries and boot hills, instead of running ranches, loving their wives, and hugging their children. Over two generations had been lost in bloody range wars that soaked into the land, and that coming on the heels of the worst war the nation had ever seen.

He closed his eyes. Gunfighter against gunfighter was not the logical way. But perhaps, like in the case of a rabid dog, the only answer was a bullet. He hurt too bad to even try to reason further with her. Later perhaps, when his body was free of the pain racking it, he could talk her out of this business.

"You still making it?" she asked.

"Doing fine," he lied.

The sun slipped behind the towering wall of the Big-horns. The day's heat slipped fast from the basin as the dun plodded on. They'd stopped once, and she had given him a slug of whiskey from the new bottle in his saddle-bags that he had forgotten was there. The liquor numbed him enough so that the ride wasn't as torturous as they wound up the canyon under the scrub pine in the twi-light.

"Your folks going to miss you?" he asked, worried he might alarm her people if she didn't return by dark.

"Nope, I spend lots of nights out on the range when I check stock and can't get back by dark."

"Fine." He fought the pitch of the frame as they started a steeper hill and the dun labored upward under the load of the travois. He thought about how now he could sell Dunny to a squaw, since the horse was already broken to pull her kind of rig. Squaw Horse might be Dunny's new name.

"We're almost there," she said, and rode her bay by his horse.

It couldn't come fast enough for him. He closed his eyes as a coyote's moaning howl broke the night's si-lence. At least he wasn't bait for coyotes, thanks to her efforts.

'We're here," she finally announced, and he awoke with a start. "Here, I'll help you up if you can walk inside. I've got a bunk ready for you."

"I must have been passed out," he said, and clenched his teeth. She bent over and took him in her arms, and he strained to help her. She proved tough and wiry, eas-ing him up on his feet in a bear hug. Then she was beside him, supporting and herding him toward the lighted open doorway.

He made it to the bunk; she eased him down. Then she lifted his boots on the bed and smiled.

"Now I'll make some beans and coffee for us."

"Sure," he said, hardly able to keep his sore eyes open.

"You want another slug of whiskey?" she asked, looking concerned at him as she leaned her forearm on the upper bunk.

"Save it. I might hurt worse later."

"True. I'll get that food cooking." With that she left him, and he stared up at the rope squares laced under the mattress above him. The world slipped away and he fell into a troubled sleep.

3

Sunlight slipped in the small glazed window on the far side of the cabin. He sat up with enough thunderous pain to make him grimace.

Then he swung his legs over to the floor. Time to get up, he decided, and rose unsteadily. She'd removed his boots sometime after he went to sleep.

His Colt was beside the bed on the top of the trunk. Not seeing her, he headed for the door, then spotted a note on the table.

Slocum

Have gone to get Nat and some others. Someone will be back shortly to check on you.

Jen

In his stocking feet he went outside, and emptied his bladder from the edge of the wooden-board stoop. Cool air swept his beard-stubbled face as he considered all the aches and pains in his body. That bunch had done a helluva good job of convincing him of something. Finished, he refastened his pants and savored the freshness of the mountain air.

A pungent turpentine smell of pines rode heavy in the stiff breeze. He lifted his gaze to the towering Bighorns that rose in the golden light of the new sun. It was some country, and he was just getting to the good part. Up this Powder River there was plenty of grass. A couple days ride north was where the Sioux and their allies had slain old Custer and his men one fateful June afternoon about nine years earlier. This country had been full of buffalo then. It was surely worth fighting over when you'd been run out of the sacred Black Hills by gold prospectors and the government.

He decided some food might be good, then turned and went back inside to see what there was to eat. He found coffee, and water in a pail. With effort, he knelt down and stoked the sheet-iron stove with the available fuel from the box nearby. He struck a lucifer on the stove top and set the kindling to blazing. Then, when he was satisfied with the fire, He set the coffeepot on to boil and went looking for something to cook.

In a tin canister he found some rice and a can of tomatoes to season it with. As he was busy putting water in a pan of water to cook the rice, he heard horses. In a few steps, he had the six-gun in his hand and had moved to the door.

"Hey, Slocum!" a familiar voice called out. "You old he-dog, get out here."

He lifted the door latch and watched tall broad-shouldered Nat Champion dismount from a big white horse. There was no mistaking the mahogany-brown mustache, the high-crowned Texas hat, the fancy blue rag around his neck, and the steel-bue eyes. Nathan

Champion looked every bit the older version of the kid who'd ridden the cattle trails out of Texas with him.

"Say, I hear that Furston bitch sicced her hounds on you," Nat said, tilting his hat back and grinning.

"I think they was elephants and they walked on me."

"Damn, you are a sight for sore eyes, old buddy." They shook hands, and Slocum led him inside.

"Say, hold up, I brought a poke of grub to sustain you. I thought I'd have to nursemaid you a while, as bad as Jen said you were. But I guess knowing you and how cute that tomboy is, I'd a kinda acted like a winged bird myself." Nat went for the white sack on his saddlehorn. He returned with a ring of his spur rowels and set it inside on the table.

"Good thing you got here," Slocum said. "I was down to rice and tomatoes." Slocum eased himself down on a straight-backed chair.

"She told me there wasn't much up here for you to eat and I needed to get up here and look after you. Damn, John, I'm sorry as hell you had to get beat up by them sons a bitches on my accord." He shook his head wearily as he stripped off his gloves and jumper. "Ain't real warm in here either."

"I've got the fire going. How is the cow business?"

"Got me half a start. I brought up a set of steers from Texas for a man, and for my share I got to bring along a hundred young cows of my own. Lordy, up here cows sell for ten times what they do down in the Texas brush. Then I wrangled up a brand."

"I read that in the letter. What's the brand law?" Slocum asked with a frown. He wasn't familiar with brand laws in the territory. In Texas, you simply registered a brand at the county courthouse.

"They got this organization of cattlemen up here that run the brand registry. Big-money folks, and only they can issue a brand, and they don't like anyone else to have one, think it encourages rustlers.'' Nat took the seat opposite Slocum and cocked one leg over the other.

"You've got a brand registered?'' Slocum asked.

"Finally, yes. The Bar C. But it wasn't easy, and I was concerned that I'd lose my herd before they issued me one. See, my cows had trail brands on them, and Wyoming didn't recognize that either.''

"How is it going now?''

"Big outfits give us small ranchers hell, but I think I'll survive. If I can get me about three to four hundred mother cows, I can live up here like a king. Real grass country and I don't shove easy.''

"You got a good calf crop on the ground?''

"Yes, and roundup is in three weeks. Do you think you'll be up to riding by then?''

"What can I do?''

"Well, they got a law in the territory that you can't brand cattle except during authorized roundups. That means the big outfits have a rep there to decide ownership on everything a hot iron touches.'' Nat reached to stretch his arms over his head.

"Does that get touchy?''

"Yes, and I could use a little backing. If you don't mind doing a little punching?''

"I'd be glad to. I should be well enough by then.''

"Good. Damn near forgot I've got some bacon to slice, and even some eggs if they didn't break coming up here.'' Nat scrambled to his feet to empty the food from the poke. "Here, pour us some whiskey,'' he said, and put the bottle on the table. "I figured you could use a little tonic and we could talk about the old days some.''

Slocum poured them each a couple fingers in some cups he found, and then toasted to a better day and to their reunion. The liquor helped ease some of his discomfort, and by then the cabin was full of the smell of bacon sizzling in the skillet. The coffee finally boiled, and with eggshells tossed in to settle out the grounds, Nat poured the first steaming rounds, and then set on the table plates of fried eggs, bacon, and slices of fresh rye bread he'd brought to go with the rest.

They didn't talk for a long while, busy slugging down the rich coffee between bites of the food. While both men were occupied with eating, Slocum thought about the girl Jen, and wondered if she and Nat had something going.

"Tell me about Jen," he said, poising his fork to punctuate his question.

"Pretty for being a half-boy, ain't she?" Nat shook his head over his breakfast.

"You have any claims on her?"

"She's a maverick. Might be a real challenge for you," Nat said, using the web of his right hand to stroke down his full mustache. "No, she ain't one I could ever corner up and get even halfway serious with. You might try, though." With a big knowing grin and a shake of his head, he shoveled in some more egg.

"She live at home?"

"Yes, she does. Her paw Emil was in a bad horse wreck and can't hardly ride. He's on crutches, so she does most of the cowboying for them. They've got about a hundred mother cows and a set of steers. But we all take her plumb serious, and do her bidding when she needs help, 'cause she ain't a shirker and has lots of sand in her craw."

"I sure appreciated all her effort getting me here. Guess she told you?"

"Yeah, she got to my place about midnight, woke us up, and said she'd used a travois to haul you up here. Hell, I rode old Frosty hard to get up here. I figured you were close to death."

Slocum nodded. "I was. I was damn close to it."

"I saw that right off. They sure messed up your face." He pushed back and took up his coffee cup. "Sure glad to see you. I was dreading this year's roundup up here. Hey, I can fight my own wars, but you've been around enough outfits and roundups and I don't think they can run over the two of us."

"What about this Furston woman?"

"Hell-bitch. She's got a heart colder than a glacier and meaner than a killer-wolf." Nat's eyes narrowed to slits, and Slocum could see the twitch in his friend's facial muscles.

"Don't sound like you and her have even been sociable."

"She sent her rannies up here to run my cows off the water and feed."

"I guess you tied tin cans to their tails?" Slocum said, enjoying Nat's rising anger and discomfort.

"Had me arrested once." Nat's eyes were narrowed to slits.

"What for?"

"Hell, didn't need a reason."

"They won't get a another chance to jump on me again either," Slocum said, and cradled the hot cup in his hands. The room was warming up from the fire in the stove, and the heat felt good. He'd been caught off guard, not expecting the welcome he had received from the FXT, but from this point on, they'd better come with their pants hitched up and guns loaded. He wasn't taking another thumping from the likes of them.

Nat stirred. "Say, I've got to deliver a couple of horses I sold down at the Kaycee to a rancher. Take me a day to ride down there and one to get back. Will you be all right here alone?"

"Nothing to do but heal. I guess she let Dunny out to graze?"

"Yes, I seen a big dun horse out there. There's good

water in the tank and you can get drinking water there. The owner put in a pipe to carry the stream.''

"Who owns this place?"

"Bucky Hurd. He's gone back to Iowa to see about some business. He sold his small herd last fall. But his claim to this place is sound and he'll be back when he settles an estate. We all kinda look after it so it don't get torched while he's gone.'' Nat rose to his feet. "I hate leaving you up here all busted up, but that money from these ponies will help me through this year.''

"Ride easy, I'll be fine,'' Slocum assured him as they went to the door.

"Nicky Ray's my cowhand. Aw, he's just a button, but he tries. He'll bring you up some more grub in a couple of days if I ain't back.'' Nat saluted Slocum from horseback, and reined the big white horse around to leave.

Slocum dug out a small cigar and lighted it. He watched Nat disappear in the scrub pines. He drew deep on his smoke and wondered about the head of the FXT. *Imagene*. She owed him for the beating and he aimed to pay her back. Sometime he would straighten her fancy butt out. He blew a small stream of smoke out from between his lips. Roundup sounded like it would be more like a small war. Before it was over, he intended to teach her and her whole crew some better manners.

He winced at the stiffness in his body and drew again on the cigar.

In a few weeks, he would be healed. A saucy jay scolded him from a nearby juniper. He smiled at its chattering. Welcome to Wyoming and the Powder River country. It'd been a helluva greeting so far.

4

Nat and the Ray boy who worked for him had both made trips up to the shack with grub and whiskey to keep Slocum supplied. He had mended enough to reset the plates on Dunny, and was splitting his own cooking wood. In fact, he saw little reason to stay up on the mountain, except that he was enjoying the solitude of the setting and welcomed the peace and quiet. Not having seen the tomboy Jen to even thank her for all her troubles, and without any knowledge of where her headquarters was, he waited. He wondered if she would ever come by to check on his condition, and perhaps the notion that she might pay him a social call was the reason he hadn't ridden down to Nat's place. There would still be time to do that.

Now, water pail in hand, he whistled as he started up the trail for the tank, watching a few robins scurry about under the pines. He had seen a mule deer or two nearby, and planned to add one to his larder. With most of the hard soreness gone, he felt ready to dress one.

He reached the large rock tank, with the rusty pipe pouring the contents of the walled-up source of water into it. Leaning over, he swung the pail under the spout as he listened to the songbirds.

The flat slap of a bullet, inches from him, brought him to awareness as the water sprayed in his face. He dropped the handle in haste and dove for his life as the second round ricocheted off the tank rim above him. Damn, they'd been close. He tried to make himself as flat as he could, thinking about the trajectory of the rounds. Snaking around on his belly with his .44 in his hand, he knew the shooter had used a rifle and that the distance between him and the ambusher made his handgun a poor weapon. Still, he wanted a chance to return some fire at the backshooter. Damn, he had gotten too careless thinking this place was so isolated and secure.

He tried to listen for any telltale sounds, but there was only the hush of the wind in the pines, and then the birds, over their fright from the shots, began singing again. The best plan was to make the ambusher think he was hit hard, and maybe he would have a chance to take the man when he ventured up to check on him. Slocum had more time than anything else since he was unscathed.

How many were out there?

Time clicked away. Nothing gave him any ideas about the shooter's whereabouts. Maybe he had taken his shots and ridden on, satisfied that he had hit Slocum. Not likely. And being cautious wasn't a bad idea. Still, Slocum had not heard a horse or a boot heel or even a cough. He waited, lying on his stomach, the warm sun soaking in his clothes and heating his back in a pleasure-filled way. The minutes ticked by.

Then a horse snorted and blew hard. His face was in the dirt where he could not see the animal, but he knew his patience would soon pay off. Someone was coming. He could hear the click of iron horseshoes on rocks and hard ground. The horse was coming uphill, through the pines. One horse was all he could make out, so he listened harder. A single animal was coming up the grade.

"Whoa."

He lay still as the sounds of boots came up the steep hillside to the flat where he lay. With the Colt in his hand, the muscles in his forearm twitched as he waited.

"Damn," the shooter muttered, and huffed, short of breath. "There you are. Guess you won't bother stealing any more of my cattle."

It was a woman. The sounds of her levering in a fresh round in her rifle sent him into a fury and he exploded. On his feet, he tackled her about the knees and sent the long gun flying from her hands. They rolled over and over, plunging downhill in each other's grip. As they finally slammed against a pine tree, he caught sight of her drawing back a gloved hand and then driving a fist into his sore face.

Damn her! He returned the favor, but knew his knuckles had missed most of her. Hat gone, her bun half undone, she had a wave of hair covering her left eye. She brushed it aside with halfhearted success. Her flushed face blazed in red anger, and she began to bombard him with her fists. He managed to raise up, and tackled her again in a bear hug to stop her fury. Locked in each other's hold, they tumbled down the mountain over more rocks and limbs. Rage was growing in his chest when they finally landed on flat ground and he pinned her shoulders down and tried to catch his breath.

"I should have killed you," she raged, and thrashed her legs in protest as he sat astride her.

He looked into her hard gray eyes, filled with fire and contempt, and it caused him to grin. The set of her tight mouth compressed until it wrinkled her thin lips. Inhaling through his nose, he considered what he'd do with her. Then he bent over and kissed her.

She tried to twist away, but under his weight all she could do was squirm and make sounds of protest behind her tightly closed mouth. Then her lips parted and he tasted the fiery honey. He raised himself to take a portion of his weight from her stomach. His hand finding the handle of her small Colt, he jerked it out and tossed it far enough away that she couldn't use it on him.

It was one thing to kiss a hellcat, another thing to trust her. She might be using all this compliance to get him to lower his guard. When he let her arms free, she soon had his face in her hands, hungry for more of his mouth, and he began undoing her holster, then found the buttons on her blouse. When his hand sought her small hard breasts, she sighed aloud with her eyes closed tight in pleasure. They stopped kissing and caught up with their breathing.

"Well, what's keeping you?" she asked, raising up on her elbows and frowning at him in some disgust. "If you're going to do it, do it!"

"Fine," he said, undoing his fly and shoving his pants down.

She lay on her back, toed off her boots, and then kicked off her long skirt, baring her smooth stomach, hips, the dark triangle, and her shapely white legs. He came between them, ready to comply with her bitchy demands, and with a deliberately hard effort, enough to make her squirm in discomfort, he thrust himself inside her.

"Yes," she said as a small grin of pleasure turned up her hard-set mouth. On cue, he pushed in further. Then she pulled him down on top of her as he sought her deepest insides in piston strokes. She wanted it rough, he'd give her what for and see who came out the winner. Besides, he owed her plenty of hard treatment.

He tried to drive her up the hillside. His knees scrambled on the gritty gravel as he worked harder and harder to meet her rising fever. She lifted her hips to receive him, and began to moan. Their fury increased, he bent over her, grasping both cheeks of her hard butt in his hands, and sought to punch himself completely through her.

Then she slumped and fainted into a limp rag. Like a windmill in a slow breeze, he kept pumping her until her eyelids finally parted and her mouth fell open in a gasp.

"Oh, God, don't stop," she gushed.

"I won't," he said.

With newfound fury, he increased his actions, and she soon caught up with him again, wrapping her legs around him. In their headlong flight, they raced like a tornado twisting and tearing across the Kansas prairie, until finally he made a final drive into her and then they both fell into a pile, exhausted and spent.

"You must come to work for me." She was sitting up beside him. Absently, as if in a dream, she twisted a button on his shirtfront.

"No."

"I can pay you—"

"We're enemies, remember? Not thirty minutes ago you tried your damnedest to kill me." He rose to a sitting position and shook his head in disbelief.

"That was before." She rose to her feet and brushed her bare ass to get rid of the dirt and needles. Then she sat back down on the ground again with a look of hopelessness. Squirming, she pulled the blouse together over her small pointed breasts capped with pale pink nipples, and began to rebutton it. Next, with a wary head shake, she held up her dirt-smudged skirt to examine it, then looked at him for an answer.

"No, we've already chosen sides." He shook his head, standing up and redoing his pants.

"Damn, you're stubborn, aren't you? I must be a hel-luva sight. I'm covered with dirt and nasty pine nee-dles." She rose to her feet again, brushing more grit and twigs off her shapely thighs and legs in an obvious show for his sake. Finally, with a loud sigh, she stepped into her skirt, bent over with an exposure of her bare butt, pulled the garment up, and then tucked in her skirt. In a sweep, she picked up her empty holster and buckled it around her waist. Dropping to the ground again, she labored to pull on her handmade boots.

"What do you want anyway?" she asked.

"I just come up here to help a friend."

"Your name is John Slocum, right?"

"Yes, and you said your name was Imagene Fur-ston."

"My friends call me Gene." She searched around the hillside for any more of her things that might have been scattered in their tussle.

"Miss Farston?"

"I'm damn sure not married." She glared at him.

"Shame," he said, rubbing his hurting chest. Wres-tling down the slope with her had loosened up his ribs, and they would be sore all over again.

"What do you mean?"

"A bedful of a woman like you needs a good man."

"You think you're so damn good?" The fury of her rage edged into her tanned face as she fought her hair back into the bun behind her head.

"No, ma'am, I sure don't."

"Hmm," she sniffed, and started up the hill. Without pins to hold it in place, her hair unrolled down her back as she stomped up the hillside. She turned once with him on her heels, gave him a scowl of contempt, and then stalked on up the slope. She swept up her black hat, and he picked up her Colt. Then, glaring at her, he punched the bullets out of the revolver one at a time while they met each other's gaze.

"Not taking any chances," he said, walking over and shoving the gun deep in her holster, so hard he forced her to lean close to his face.

"So you're going to help these rustlers?" she asked.

"I'm going to help my friends round up their cattle."

She held a fist in her other hand as if she was trying to keep from hitting him. He looked down at the top of her dusted hat crown, and could almost hear her breath raging through her thin nose. If she didn't explode again, he would be surprised.

What the hell. He might as well finish this off with a kiss. He swept her in his arms. Bent over, spilling her hat, he lifted her up in his arms, off her feet, then kissed her hard, unyielding mouth and felt her rock-hard breasts buried into his chest. She finally managed to pry herself loose and regain her feet. Her eyes became burning brands as she glared up at him.

"Gawdamn you saddle tramp, I'm not your whore!"

"Ride easy," he said, recovering her stiff hat by the brim and handing it to her. There was no need for him to reply to her anger. She'd become uncomfortable with the fragile line they'd both crossed.

Defiantly, she snatched it away from him, then stomped off to her horse. He stood on the hill and watched her mount the black. Then, without a glance back at him, Imagene Furston rode off the mountain.

He found his .44, holstered it and went to see about the pail. Empty enough to float, the bucket rode in the tank. He recovered it and filled it under the spout. Then he searched for his hat. Finding it downhill, he brushed off the worst pine needles and debris. A little shaken by the course of events, he combed his hair back with his fingers and replaced the Stetson. Damn, all he was up there for was to fetch a pail of water.

Whistling "Oh, Susanna," he went back to the cabin with the full bucket in hand. Some days were like this, but he hadn't expected such treatment at the base of the Bighorns. He pursed his tender lips and began to whistle.

5

"You ready to become civilized?" Jenny Van Doren rode up on a roan with a warm smile on her freckled face. "You been up here long enough. I figure you must be about ready to toot your horn."

He set down the ax. The firewood stack was piled head high and split enough to suit him. The exercise had helped heal his soreness. Somehow, he hadn't remembered Jen's freckles, but they added something else appealing to her.

"Actually, I took a liking to this place. So much that when Buck comes back, I may try to trade him out of it."

"You kinda beat all." She shook her head as if amused at his words. "I asked Nicky Ray the other day if you were ever coming down, and he shrugged at me. Said I better come up here and tell you there were lots of good folks down at Buffalo that ain't like the FXT bunch. In fact, they don't even like them rannies no way.

31

That bunch stays mostly down at Powder River crossing where you stopped and got the wrong directions.''

''I understand I asked at the wrong place. Must be close to lunchtime,'' he said, checking the sun. ''We'll have some of that venison I've got cooking, then I'll pack up and go down the mountain with you.''

''Sounds great. I could eat some,'' she said, dropping off her horse and slipping off the bridle so the horse could graze. She hung it on the horn and wrapped the reins up so they wouldn't drag. ''Now you're loose, Joe, don't you go and roll with my saddle on,'' she warned the cow pony before hitching up her jeans in a hop, then going with Slocum to the shack.

''Getting close to roundup?'' he asked as he waited for her to wash at the pan on the table outside the door.

''Close. Do you know that old stuffy Major Wolcott they're sending up here to over see the branding?''

''He military?'' he asked, stepping over to the pan to scrub his hands next while she dried hers on the old shirt rag.

''He was once. But he still thinks he's some kind of a king. You will see. Biggest pain in the—ass. That's it. Call a spade a spade, right?'' She narrowed her eyes for an answer from him.

''Right. Sounds interesting as hell—got a major for a brand rep and plenty of hard feelings between folks working together.''

''Pure hell each year. Tell me, Slocum, you aren't a drifting cowboy. Nat says you ramrodded some big cattle drives in the seventies. Tell me your story.'' She paused in the doorway for his reply.

''I'll tell mine if you'll tell me yours,'' he said, drying his hands and grinning at her serious look.

''There ain't much to that.'' She shook her head as if she wondered why he'd even broach the matter, and went inside. ''You've got yourself a deal.''

"Let me set the food on the table and then I'll start."

"I'll get the plates and silverware. It smells good."

Between bites, he told her about Alabama, a boy growing up on a large plantation who liked hunting fishing and trapping more than he did books. But his parents insisted on the learning business despite his wishes to be out riding or chasing hounds. He told her about his boyhood, things he had not thought about in years.

"Your family had slaves?" she asked, sitting back with a sigh from being too full.

"Field slaves, house servants, we had the whole thing," he said, then rose to fetch the coffeepot.

"Did you whip them?"

"I never did. I can remember hearing them singing in the fields, picking cotton. I guess it was what you'd call the innocence of growing up. I can't remember many bad things about life there. We all had plenty to eat, lots of laughter with the slaves, and everyone on the place smiled. I think the thunder that changed everything was the first cannons I heard in the war," he said, refilling her cup.

"You were in the war?"

"That's not the good part," he said with a grim shake of the head.

"But Nat said that you—"

"The South that I knew was over after Lee surrendered. So I drifted west afterwards and tried my hand at lots of things. Cattle driving to Kansas was a good business for a few years." He scraped off their plates and then dumped them in a dishpan to scald in the hot water on the dry sink. Satisfied that they were clean enough, he dried them one at time with a rag and replaced them on the shelf.

"You never settled down?" she asked.

"You mean married with kids?" he asked her with a grin as he tossed out the water.

"Yes, those kinds of things," she said, and slumped down in the chair, casting her boots out under the table with a ring of spur rowels.

"Never tied the knot." He took a chair opposite her.

"Just drifted, huh?" She folded her arms over her bustline.

"If we had our lives to live over, we'd all probably do them differently."

"I kinda like mine the way it is, but it's sure simple compared to all the things you've done and seen, I guess."

"That's why I told you gunfighters weren't the answer. I've seen the destruction they can cause."

"Yeah, but she and them big outfits hired them first." Jen looked hard at him for an answer.

"War's war. Can't no one win."

"I been sitting here thinking about all that you've told me," she said, gazing down at the tabletop. "You're running from something, aren't you?"

"I told you once, we'd all like to redo our mistakes and live differently." He lifted his cup and sipped the last of the coffee. Lord, if he could retrace his life, he would probably be settled on his own place in the Texas hill country, or ranching in the alpine meadows of northern New Mexico. He closed his eyes for a moment, thinking about the alternatives, before a vision appeared of the brown poster with one thousand dollars reward and a resemblance to his face and his name on it. "Contact the sheriff in Ft. Scott, Kansas," it said. He sat up straight in the chair and drew a deep shuddering breath to shake off the ill thoughts.

"Slocum, I ain't never made a big mistake. This might be a big one. Do you think I'm ugly?"

"No."

"Good!" She bolted out of the chair and drew in a

deep breath, leaning over the table with both hands on top of it. "We best be going."

"Something wrong?" he asked.

"Who really are you?"

"Jen, your momma ever warn you about a class of men in this world?"

"Yes, gamblers and slick talkers."

"I'm one of them," he said, and went to roll up his bedroll.

"I can't say you haven't warned me." She put her weathered hat on and cinched the chin strap tight.

He glanced over as she leaned with one hand on the doorway and looked across the pines and over the wide basin to the far-off purple mountains. Nice-looking girl. Why hadn't Nat and she gotten serious? His roll tight and tied, he took it to his saddle and then picked up the bridle.

"We going?" he asked, stopping behind her as she blocked the doorway.

She turned and looked him over from head to toe. Then, with a shrug, she took the bridle from him.

"I'll get old Dunny for you. You bring your gear."

"Jen, we leave something unsaid?" he asked after her as she headed out in her rocking gait across the yard. She sure had a cute backside, all sandwiched in those tight britches and exposed out of the back of her chaps.

She turned and wrinkled her pert nose at him. Then, as if she had thought on it, she said, "It can wait, Slocum."

"Good," he said, and hefted the saddle and gear to his shoulder as he closed the door.

The town of Buffalo looked good enough to him in the twilight. It was at the base of the Bighorns, and they rode up the narrow street with lights from the various businesses spilling across the boardwalks. The smell of sour whiskey and stale cigar smoke seeped out of various saloons into the night air. Tinny piano music drifted out, and the loud haughty laughter of a soiled dove carried to him as they rode past. Their horses drummed over the hollow-sounding bridge that spanned the gurgling creek. Cow ponies stood hipshot in rows at the hitch racks. They finally stopped before a cafe.

"Only place they'll let single ladies in," she said with a curl of her upper lip, and then she dismounted.

He searched around and then, out of habit, adjusted the six-gun in his holster. She led the way inside, and several customers called out to her as she went to an empty table.

"Myra," she said to the tall girl in the white apron who had come over to wait on them. "This is Nat's good friend Slocum."

"Nice to meet you, sir."

"We want two big steaks if they weren't cut off a bear, and a side of potatoes, plenty of bread and butter," Jen ordered. "And bring on the coffeepot."

Myra looked at him for his approval, and he nodded.

"I guess I should have asked you first what you wanted?" She looked around and then rose to her feet. "They've got a place to wash up out back."

"Lead the way," he said.

Several punchers acknowledged her and a few asked her about her paw as they worked their way to the rear of the diner and went out through a kitchen full of rich food smells. On the back porch with only the light of the open door falling on the porch, she rolled up her sleeves and went to scrubbing her hands and forearms with a bar of homemade soap. He leaned against the wall and waited.

"Ain't a man in there ever asked you to a dance?" he asked with a head toss.

"What?" she asked, whipping the towel away from

her face to look at him in wide-eyed disbelief.

"All them cowboys in there and you haven't got one?"

"Why, I wouldn't have the whole lot of them," she scoffed.

"Who you looking for?"

"I don't see that's none—"

"Wait, I recall we have this trade. I told you all about my life."

"Nothing happened in mine," she said, and dropped her gaze.

"Not one of them ever asked you to a dance?" He peeled back his cuffs to wash his hands.

"Dammit, I ain't looking for no sugar-foot bum." She kicked the table leg and made the wash pan careen around like a tossed saucer, spilling water on the countertop. "Sorry. Why don't I appeal to Nat or a real man?"

"How do you know that you don't?"

"Hell, he's like the rest of you." She lowered her voice. "Wave me away, then turn their back on me and piss like a stud horse and never expect I have any feelings."

"I'd've never done that if I hadn't been so damn beat up." He reached for the towel, but she snatched it away to hold his attention.

"I know that, but you weren't the only one. Most times they think I'm a damn boy like Nicky." Then she handed him the towel to dry himself on.

"No one kisses boys either," he said softly.

"Oh, hell, I can testify to that." She looked to the starry sky for help.

"Come on, I'm ready for a real steak." He placed his hand on her shoulder and guided her inside. He grinned to himself, following her as she went in her rocking gait through the kitchen and then back to their table. There was more woman in that package than anyone knew, he realized.

He had just sat down when he heard someone swear out loud. Her eyes widened about something behind him, and he rose as his chair clattered to the floor. On his heels, he whirled to face the flush-faced cowboy with the blue rag wrapped around his chicken neck. Slocum knew the FXT man.

"We told you to get the hell out—"

"You giving the orders in here?" Slocum asked. He wondered if the other man with him was one of Furston's bunch.

"I say you're another damn rustler!" The man was drunk enough to slur his words.

"Let's go outside and settle this," Slocum said. "There are gentlefolks in here."

"Hell, I'll meet you anywhere."

"Outside." Slocum pointed as the other younger rider whispered something to the drunk ranny.

"I can whip the shit out of him anywhere," the ranny said. Then someone said in a hushed voice that the drunken puncher's name was Luke. Meanwhile, his friend hustled Luke out the door.

"Be careful," Jen whispered.

Slocum acknowledged her warning and strode out in the street.

Luke was standing on unsteady boot heels, beyond the hitched horses, in the center of the dark street. He drew up his fists, stuck out his jaw, and waved at Slocum to join him in what would hardly resemble a Marquis of Queensberry competition.

Slocum stepped into the street, handing Jen his hat. In two long strides he moved in. Working in sideways and leading with his left fist, he began jabbing at Luke. Luke swung wild, and left an opening that Slocum used to drive two hard blows to the man's gut and force the air from his solar plexus. Then he used a powerful punch to connect with the bent-over cowpuncher's jaw, and sent him reeling backwards into the string of ponies behind him.

The confusion of the arm-waving fighter piling into their midst caused some of the sleeping horses to awaken suddenly, and the snap of leather reins sent some of their owners to shouting to calm them down. This caused more mounts to spook, and to save himself from being trampled, the addled Luke was forced to crawl as fast as he could for the far boardwalk.

"Here's your hat," Jen said, handing it to Slocum. "Your supper's getting cold."

He dropped a hand on her shoulder and squeezed it. He knew she was looking up at him as they both headed back for the cafe. Luke was a hard-jawed sum-bitch. His right hand hurt like fire.

6

"Morning, fellas. I need to ride up and gather up some of my horses to use on the roundup," Nat explained when he rode up to the Van Doren Ranch. "A bunch of them are up past the old fort. A granger said he saw them up there last week. I thought you might like to tag along. Slocum?" He dismounted in front of the barn where he'd found Slocum and Jen's father, Emil, busy shoeing horses.

"I'll be ready to ride in a few minutes," Slocum said, straightening up from tacking a shoe on Jen's bay.

"You figure they got up there natural-like?" Emil Van Doren asked as he looked at his dusty boot toes and hung his armpits on his crutches. The elder Van Doren had trailed around the ranch after Slocum as he tried to lend Jen a hand to get caught up on things.

"Emil, I ain't sure of anything anymore," Nat said, stroking his mustache. "Say, everyone in town is talking about that stupid FXT puncher Luke trying to spar with

40

the master there." He pointed accusingly at Slocum for the older man's benefit.

Slocum shook his head to dismiss the talk as he bent over to file off the nail points in the horse's hoof. Finished, he straightened, pleased that he didn't have to shoe horses for a living.

"There, old Joe's hooves look a lot better," Jen said, joining them under the side shed.

"He should do to ride. I reset them," Slocum explained. "I'm going to go up with Nat and bring back his string of horses."

"Don't you two rowdies get in any fights up there," Jen said as she joined them. "The sheriff locked old Luke up last night for starting that fight with Slocum, and it cost Miss Furston's foreman thirty bucks to bail him out."

"Where did you hear all that?" Nat asked with a frown.

"Old Fred Gulley rode by about an hour ago and told me all about it."

"I swear, girl, you can learn more out here than I can learn all day in town."

"I can't help, Nat, that folks like to talk to me," she said, and then she led Joe off, pausing to turn and warn them, "Oh, yes, don't forget your slickers. It's going to rain."

"Rain, my ass," Nat said under his breath. "There ain't a cloud in the sky. Emil, where does she get a crazy notion that it's going to rain?"

"I never know," he said mildly, and then thanked Slocum for his help before he drew himself up on the crutches and headed for the house.

Slocum saddled Dunny and got busy getting his things tied down. He made no comment on the girl's prediction, more amused by Nat's reception to the warning than anything else.

"Rain? For crimany sakes, there ain't a thing to forecast that by. Almanac probably said it would rain from now till the end of the month. Ah, hell.'' Nat rambled on about her weather-forecasting as they rode out along the long lane, past the small field of greening alfalfa behind the A-frame post fence.

They weren't five miles from the Van Doren Ranch when the sky over the Bighorns became filled with thick dark clouds, and soon the storms moved into the basin. Without a word, Slocum undid his slicker from behind his cantle.

"How do you reckon did she knew that was coming?" Nat asked, tilting his head to the side as he drew on his raincoat.

"I'd say maybe you should take that girl more serious."

"Jenny Van Doren?" He squinted his eyes at Slocum, then shook his head in disbelief.

Thunder rolled overhead, and the first drops of hard rain struck their hats and ran down the rubber-sheeted slickers. It would be a long ride to recover his horses. Slocum settled in the saddle. Cold and wet was his forecast for the rest of the day.

"We couldn't find a herd of elephants in this weather," Nat complained as the thunderous downpour continued. "Let's head up to Story and get us a room at Chelsey's. My fingers look like dried prunes.'' He held up his wrinkled fingers as proof.

Slocum agreed, and they turned to the northwest, pushing their horses into the storm's force. He could hardly see the face of the Bighorns, except when the clouds parted briefly in their fast-moving path. Then more lightning and hard rain battered them. He felt certain that whatever was at the town of Story and Chelsey's would beat being out in this weather. Unless they stumbled on top of Nat's ponies, they'd never find them in this mess.

Arriving in Story, they dismounted at a stable and led their horses inside the dark alleyway, grateful to be out of the weather pelting the shingle roof above them. Both men loosened their girths.

"Howdy," a whiskered stable man said, coming out of the office with a lantern held up to see their faces.

"Need to put these ponies up," Nat told the man.

"Yes, siree, she's coming a flood, ain't she?" He hung the light on a hook and drew out a stub of a pencil to mark down their names.

"Sure is. My name's Nat Champion."

"I knowed you, what's his?"

"Slocum."

"You spell that with one g or two g's?" The man licked the lead and waited, poised to scribble it down on his pad.

"One's enough," Slocum said with a smile. "You got grain?"

"Cost two bits extra."

"Feed them."

"You fellas planning to leave them long?"

"Hope for only one day," Nat said.

"Well, I guess they're good enough horseflesh that I could get my board bill out of them if you forget where they are."

"We won't forget them," Nat assured the man.

Then they headed out in the blowing sheets of precipitation for the saloon and hotel up the street. The boardwalk was slick with water, and the footing was close to treacherous under their wet leather soles. They managed to reach the saloon's porch without falling, then entered the left side of the double doors and stepped inside the warm room. Both bat-wing shutters were tied back. The rich smell of sour-mash distillery products filled the heated air, and a veil of cigar smoke hung head high. A few cardplayers looked up at them, then, uninterested, turned back to their games.

Slocum saw her eyes brighten up when they came in under the wagon-wheel lamp's light. He guessed her age, maybe eighteen. With dark wavy hair, she looked a cut above the average girls who worked in such places. Her full breasts looked like two fat white piglets about to escape the top of her frilly black dress as she came swinging over to greet them.

"Howdy, I'm Etta. Welcome to Chelsey's," she said, beaming as she blocked their way.

"Why, howdy, Etta," Nat said with a grin wide as the Rio Grande, and swept off his hat. "I'm Nat Champion, and this here's my pard Slocum."

"Nice to meetcha, ma'am," Slocum said, and removed his rain-sodden Stetson.

"Thanks." She smiled and winked her brown eyes wickedly at the two of them. "You boys want a table, whiskey, some food?"

"I'd take anything," Nat said. "Where can we hang these slickers?"

"I'll take them and put them on a peg over on the wall."

"They'll get you all wet," Slocum said, concerned.

"No problem, I dry fast," she said, and took one slicker in each hand. En route she expertly avoided a playful slap on the rump from one of the cardplayers.

"Etta, why don't you hang up my coat?" a man in glasses across the table asked.

"Because," she said with a sashay of her hips, "you ain't a gentleman."

"Gentleman!" the man under the derby snorted. "Them two look like ordinary cowpunchers to me," he complained, and then discarded two cards.

''No class,'' she said, shaking her head as she came back to Slocum and Nat's table.

''What'll it be, gents?'' she said, leaning over their table with both hands down on the scarred top. Slocum looked at the view and thought it was interesting.

''A bottle of good bonded rye,'' he said, meeting her gaze.

''And you?'' She looked at Nat.

''A couple of thick steaks and a platter of potatoes. You want one?'' he asked her pointedly.

''Can I nibble on yours?'' she asked, and wrinkled her nose a little to dismiss any concern he had for her hunger.

''Damn right you can,'' he said, about ready to jump up.

''Rye and *three glasses*?'' She searched them for the answer.

''Yes, some good rye and three glasses,'' Slocum said.

''Then I'll order the steaks for you two.''

''We'll need a room for tonight too,'' Nat said as she started for the bar.

She turned, looked right at him as she licked her pouty lips with the tip of her tongue, and then held up two fingers. There was no mistaking her meaning.

''Yes, ma'am, we need two rooms,'' Nat agreed as he smiled after her exit.

''New girl, I take it?'' Slocum asked, digging out small cigars for both of them. He struck a lucifer under the table and torched Nat's, then his own.

''Yes, and she sure is nice.'' Nat shook his head as if he couldn't believe their luck.

In a minute, she returned and placed the whiskey on the table along with three glasses. Slocum had to admit to himself he plain liked the way her breasts jiggled— she sure wasn't bad.

"Now I'm going to turn in your orders for the food," she whispered. "Don't you two drink all of it while I'm gone."

"We won't," Nat promised her quietly.

"I'll reserve those rooms then too," she whispered.

"Good," he said, and then cleared his throat.

What the hell were they talking softly for? Slocum had a hard time suppressing his amusement. Still, he had to admit something about her took his breath away, and all this acting she did was sure working on Nat as well. He watched her swing her fine ass crossing the room—not your plain old Barroom Sally at all.

He reached over and poured two half glasses of the amber rye. Then he slouched back in the chair. He raised his glass in a silent toast. *Here's to Etta and a hundred like her.* The whiskey proved smooth and he sipped it slowly, enjoying the warmth of the room and the escape from the thundering rain outside.

"I guess you ain't seen Imagene since her crew whipped the hell out of you," Nat said.

"I didn't tell you, did I?"

"No." Nat frowned. "Did they come back and try again?"

"She did."

"What happened?"

"I'd sort of call it a draw that time." Slocum raised his glass in a toast.

"Which one of you buckeroos wants me to sit in his lap?" Etta asked, back from her tasks.

"Me!" Nat shouted, and nearly fell over backwards frowning at Slocum's words as he tried to slide his chair back from the table and make room for her.

"Good," she said, gathering up her skirt and taking a place in Nat's lap. "I wasn't breaking in on anything important, was I?" She removed his hat and smoothed his hair, then replaced the hat.

"No, ma'am." Slocum grinned and filled a tumbler with four fingers of rye for her. He moved it across the table toward her, and then he noticed how much that Nat was enjoying her close company.

7

In the early morning, Slocum stood on Chelsey's porch and watched the sun break through the remaining clouds. The street was a sea of mud, split by an elegant rig's thin wheels as it passed. Fancy horses stepped out and the driver barely looked his way, but from the fancy Prince Albert coat, ruffled white shirt, and cravat, he looked very self-important. Finished with his cigar, Slocum gave the butt a high arc and it sizzled in a mud hole. He considered the roof of the porch and their quarters upstairs. Nat and Etta had kept him awake most of the night in the room next to him.

Slocum decided it had been long enough and that the cook back in the rear kitchen would have the coffee done by now. At the door, he stopped to observe the three men who rode by at a trot. He looked harder at them as he stood back in the porch's shadows. One he knew well. The big Scotsmen McEntosh who worked for Imagene Furston was the center rider. He knew that none of them had seen him as he slipped inside the saloon. He was not particularly afraid of the three. He simply wanted to meet them on his own terms in some place of privacy, but he'd have time for that later.

"There he is!" Etta said with her arms wrapped around Nat as they started down the stairs. "I told you he hadn't left without you."

Slocum waited for the two of them.

"You ready to ride?" Nat asked behind his bleary sleep-deprived eyes.

"I am. If you promise not to fall off your horse."

"Oh, Slocum, he never falls off," she said, and rolled her eyes back to look at the ceiling for help.

"That's good, because we have to find his ponies and get on to roundup."

"I know. I'm going to get to come down there and help," she announced as they crossed the barroom for the back room. "Nat said that I could. Didn't you?"

"Sure."

"Some day I'm going to have a ranch of my own and own lots of cattle," she said. "You believe me, don't you, Slocum?"

"Yes, ma'am," he said, holding the kitchen door open for them.

"Some day I'm going to have lots of cows and calves under my own brand," she said, and went for cups for them, pointing to a table and chairs at the side. "We can sit there and eat our breakfast."

She went over and put her arm on the cook's shoulder as he stood over the stove. "I want some eggs over easy. How about you, Slocum?" she asked without turning.

"Cooked is fine with me."

"Nat, honey?" She half turned, still leaning on the older man's frame.

"Any way you like them, little darling." Nat grinned and then stuck out his chest.

"You do his like mine," she directed the cook, leaning close while he readied a skillet on the stove top. "We want fried potatoes, ham, biscuits, lots of gravy. The way to a man's heart is through his belly, my momma told me."

She sauntered over to the table beaming like a pup who had just rounded up the last cow. "You'll see, Slocum. I can ride like a man and I'm sure going to be in the cattle business myself."

"Why, Etta, I never doubted you for a minute."

She dropped in the chair and pawed Nat. "He don't either, do you, Nat?"

"No, baby, but you may not like this damned old Major Wolcott that the big outfits are sending along as their rep," Nat said with a deep sigh.

"Is he a man?" She winked at Slocum.

"A grumpy old bastard."

"I can handle him, honey, trust me." She bent over to get close to his face and kiss him. Then, for good measure, she climbed on his lap.

"Oh, I trust you, darling. But Major Walcott ain't nice at all," Nat said, adjusting her and taking another quick peck on the mouth.

"He may get better," Slocum said, slouching down in his chair and wondering if old Nat was having misgivings about allowing her to go along on the roundup. Yes, sir, a good dose of her and that old major might even become tolerable. Though Slocum had never met the man, by his reputation from what Nat and Jen had told him, he was crusty as a double-cooked pie.

They ate breakfast, paid their bill, and after more kissing between her and Nat, the two men went after their horses. Neither of them spoke as they hurried down the boardwalk in the shadowy coolness of the early morning.

"Morning, Mr. Champion. You must be Slow-gun?" the boy asked, reading the paper. "A big dun back there?"

"That's mine," Slocum said, getting his saddle off the rack in the office. Bridles in his hand, the youth left to get their mounts.

"What's McEntosh doing up here?" he asked Nat.

"He up here?" Nat frowned.

"Rode by the saloon over an hour ago with two men. Before the cook had coffee made."

"Kinda north of his range. No good, I reckon." Nat acted still half asleep as the boy returned with both animals.

"Where's this farmer live that saw your horses?" Slocum asked as he tossed on his saddle.

"Somewhere up the creek."

"Good. This where Crazy Horse killed Fetterman and his whole command?"

"Yeah, back that way a couple of miles, call it Dead Man's Hill. They suckered him over the ridge with a small party, and every Injun on this side of the ridge was loaded for bear when he committed himself."

"I came through here after that with a herd headed for the Montana gold fields. The military down at Fort Laramie wouldn't let us by. They'd shut all these forts up and down the face of the Bighorns. Red Cloud burned that one down himself, Jim Bridger told me. We bought enough cartridge rifles and ammunition for every man and the hell with them stripped legs—we drove that herd up through here." Slocum arranged the saddle pad and then set his saddle high up on Dunny's wethers.

"No problems?" Nat asked, tossing his rig on his horse and grabbing for the cinch under his belly.

"We killed a few Indians. They soon learned we had

more range with those new guns than they'd ever seen. And we never meet any big war parties like George Armstrong did later, so we were lucky.''

''Make some big money?''

''My partner and I spilt close to two thousand dollars for six months work gathering them in Texas and driving them through.''

''Damn, a thousand bucks.'' Nat swung up on his white horse. ''How long did it last?''

''Not long enough. I meet a sweet thing about like Etta and we played roulette and dined on fancy food. Had a high old time. Probably lasted about a month.''

''What did you do then?'' Nat asked as their horses plodded down the empty, muddy street.

''Went back to Texas for another stake. I think about then a wet-nosed Champion boy came along and joined a cattle drive to Kansas.''

''Yeah, wet-nosed. Say, if I had a thousand bucks today, I'd own fifty more cows.''

''I know,'' Slocum said. He looked at the towering Bighorns in the rain-cleaned air. Their peaks were still snowcapped above the purple slopes covered in pines and high meadows rising into the sky. He would have bought cows too then, but he'd had to move on anyway.

''Say, there's a roan horse of mine.'' Nat pointed to a horse in a rail corral.

''Looks like he's in that man's lot.''

''Yeah, they've got a lot of damn gall, ain't they.''

''Ride easy, it may be a mistake,'' Slocum cautioned him as they rode up to the low-roofed log cabin.

''Got my damn brand on him.''

''Howdy,'' a red-haired barefoot youth said as he came out of the house and used his hand to shade his eyes.

''That roan horse.'' Nat used his thumb to indicate him.

"Is he yours, mister?"

"He's got my brand on him."

"No one knew him up here. I thought he was strayed so I put him up. He's a nice horse."

Nat dismounted and shook his head in disgust.

"I sure never meant to make him mad," the boy said, taken back.

Slocum shook his head to dismiss the boy's concern.

"Well, gawdamn it!" Nat swore, putting a rope on the roan's neck to lead him out. "They've used Blue for a damn plow horse. He's got collar marks on his shoulders."

"He's gentle and I never hurt him working him," the boy said to Slocum.

"It didn't hurt him," Slocum said. "Nat, pay this boy for keeping your horse."

"Pay him? What for? This was a great cow pony. I can't take him to roundup looking like he come from hauling a funeral wagon." He came out of the corral leading the roan, shaking his head like he'd lost an entire war.

"Then you leave him here and let this young man have him. He ain't ashamed of the collar mark."

"Where's your folks?" Nat asked the boy.

"My mom died last spring and my paw's laid up in the cabin."

"He seen a doctor?" Slocum asked.

"He don't believe in them, sir."

"How many them young'uns in there peeking out at us?" Slocum motioned to the cabin doorway.

"Four, and the oldest is ten and the youngest is four."

"How old are you?"

"Fourteen. I mean, I will be in July. Say, my paw's calling. I need to go inside." The boy turned on his bare heels and raced to the cabin.

"Tell him to rest easy," Slocum called. "What's the name?"

"Billy Dale," the boy said, then rushed back inside the cabin.

"What you figure that roan's worth?" Slocum asked Nat.

"Forty bucks here at roundup."

"But he's got some hair rubbed off his shoulders from that collar." Slocum motioned with his right hand.

"What are you getting at?"

"I want to buy him."

"What the hell for?" Nat scowled at him.

"Me and Billy Dale is going in partnership up here."

"What would you give?"

"Twenty-five and make Billy Dale a sale bill on something after you put the roan back in the corral."

"Slocum, you make less sense than I do drunk." Nat led the horse back, shaking his head.

Billy Dale popped out of the door. Slocum tossed him two silver dollars. In disbelief, he caught them in both hands, and his green eyes flew open wide.

"You go to Story and buy a better-fitting collar for *our horse*," Slocum said. "This summer you raise a good garden. I'll be back to eat some with you."

"Yes, sir. You leaving that roan horse?" The boy squinted in disbelief.

"I can't figure how you and me are making a garden without you having him to use." He could hear the kids giggling excitedly as the word passed among them out of sight inside the door.

"Yes sir, but it will be July before—"

"You got seed?"

"Yes, sir, I do. Where can I send you word when it's getting ripe?"

"Oh, I'll be coming by when it's ready."

"And I'll watch his shoulders too."

Nat came back. "Here's the bill of sale, and I would appreciate you not telling folks you got him from Nat Champion. Tell them Slocum sold him to you."

"Say, Mr. . . . Champion." The boy read the name off the paper. "You can come by and eat some too."

"I don't eat anything but meat," Nat said, and gave a toss of his head to Slocum that he was ready to ride on.

"Tell your paw to get well, Billy Dale," Slocum said, and waved at the curious round eyes stacked up in the doorway to watch.

"I sure will, thanks. Bye, Mr. Slocum."

Slocum set his heels to Dunny and loped after Nat.

8

"I won't have a horse left to ride to roundup if every soft-soaper between here and Crazy Woman Creek has some sad story for you," Nat said under his breath. "You've given away more in your life than twenty men."

"You ever see where it's hurt me?"

"No, and I guess them poor folks back there sure needed some help." He twisted to look back.

"No guess to it, but that's not here or there. Let's find them ponies of yours and get back."

"Great country up here, isn't it?" Nat leaned back in his saddle, grasping the horn, and took in the grandeur of the mountain range towering above them.

"Beautiful," Slocum agreed. The purple face of the Bighorns stretched north and south, rising like a great wall before them as they rode up the flats. The majesty of the mountains impressed him any time he came in their view.

"You can go up in them Bighorns," Nat said, pointing at them, "and kill a moose or an elk, even a bear. There's some grizzlies still up in them peaks and they are ferocious as ten wildcats. There's mule deer with racks big as elk too."

"And, my friend, when that north wind blows," Slocum said, "I know where a senorita smokes corn-husk roll-your-owns and lives on the Guadalupe River below San Antonio, and the sun down there is a damn sight warmer than it is up here." Both men stood in their stirrups laughing at his words as they trotted their horses up the grade and into the next broad meadow.

"Don't say nothing to Jen about Etta coming to roundup," Nat said.

"No need." Slocum looked over at his uncomfortable pard.

"I'll tell her something myself." Nat pointed to the gray and red horses grazing off toward the stream as they left the wagon road and headed for them.

"Ain't much need in me telling her a thing," Slocum said. "I think she'll discover it right off."

"Dammit, when Etta found out I was going on roundup, she insisted she come along. She's a hard woman to deny anything." Nat shook his head as if he wished he had never told her that she could join them.

"I'd say so. That would be hard," Slocum agreed.

"They're all here," Nat said as they reined up and he counted the horses in silence, moving his lips through the numbers.

"Which one leads them?" Slocum asked, shaking out his lariat.

"Put a string on old Red, the chestnut." Nat pointed to the tall roman-nosed red horse.

With Nat on the outside crowding him back from escaping to the south, both men raced their mounts across the open ground after the chestnut, undoing their lariats.

Slocum's first try to rope him fell short, so he quickly reeled in his hemp as they chased the errant cow pony. As they approached the end of the meadow at a fast clip, he rebuilt his loop and wondered if the horse would make good his getaway into the scrub pines ahead before they captured him. On his second try, Slocum rose in the stirrups, whirled the loop hard, and reached out to toss it. The loop nestled over the gelding's neck. Slocum jerked the slack and then took a double wrap on the horn as he turned Dunny off to stop him. When the rope tightened, Red scooted to a sliding stop with his hind hooves under him, then, as if all his training had suddenly come home, he fell in behind Dunny. Nat went to herding the others after him.

"If we move along, we can be back home by dark," Nat said.

"You want to lead the way?"

"No, you're headed right. We'll cut across country till we hit the road."

"Sure enough." Slocum set out in a long trot, standing in his stirrups. A horse could trot for twenty miles easy, and he knew that they had more than that to cover.

Noisy killdeer raced before them searching for bugs as they rode through the brown winter-cured grass and pungent purple sagebrush. It was a good grassland and the horses had wintered well. They were shedding already and with a good curry-combing, they'd look like new again. He looked back at Nat, swinging his rope and bringing on the rest of the remuda. Be lots of explaining for his pard the way he figured it when Etta showed up for roundup. About tickled with the notion, he managed to suppress his amusement and rode on.

They stopped for noon and let the horses water in a small stream flush with runoff from the rain the day before. Nat found some crackers and cheese in his saddlebags. Both items were not from a recent purchase, but Slocum and Nat topped them off with some good whiskey from Slocum's saddlebags and a cigar apiece, then soaked up the sun, lounging on the ground while the horses grazed.

"So Miss Imagene showed up at Buck's cabin?" Nat finally got around to asking as he lay on his side, holding his head with a crooked elbow.

"She ain't a bad shot either." On his back, Slocum studied the fluffy passing clouds and the red-tailed hawk floating above on the wing, looking for a meal.

"She shot at you?"

"Since I've thought about it, I believe she shot beside me." Yes, she had not wanted to hit him hard, because then she couldn't punish him as she'd intended. Even if she did hit him hard, her original plan had been to lord it over a wounded man.

"Shot beside you? That don't make no sense."

"It makes some," Slocum said, blowing a steady stream of smoke out of his compressed lips.

"I guess it does. But I figured she was colder than winter in Alaska."

"They tell me they've got spring and summer up there. It just don't last as long."

"I'd gave a hundred bucks to have been a little bird in a tree when it was going on."

"You're pretty generous with your money. Are we about ready to ride?" Slocum asked, grinding out the butt in the dirt and tearing it apart until satisfied it would not cause a fire when they rode on.

"Has she got freckles on her butt?"

Slocum considered the question as he tightened the girth. Then he swung in the saddle. He recalled the snowy derriere as she had pulled on her divided skirt, and then shook his head. "Nope, pure-dee white."

"Figured so," Nat said, and trotted past to get around his herd.

"We've got company coming." Slocum reined his horse around and tossed his head toward the riders coming up their back trail.

"It's Sheriff Dugan and *her* bunch."

"What the hell do they want?" Slocum asked out loud, seeing the big Scotsmen and the others he had seen earlier in Story. He and Nat reined up and kept the horses in a wad as the four riders came up.

"Sheriff," Nat said with a nod, ignoring the others.

"Howdy, Nat. Don't reckon I met your friend there." The man, dressed in a brown suit with a great handlebar mustache and a Texas hat, nodded at Slocum.

"Friend of mine. What's the problem, Sheriff?" Nat asked, not bothering to introduce him.

"McEntosh here swears you butchered one of the FXT calves."

"You listening to liars these days?" Nat demanded with his hand on the butt of his gun.

"Easy, Nat," the lawman said to calm things down. "The man has a hide that he claims was in your shed, and these two men are his witnesses. I want you to peaceful-like come back to Buffalo and we'll settle this in court."

"He's the damn rustler. Do your duty and arrest him, mon," McEntosh demanded, his face turning black with rage.

"What the hell was he doing in my shed anyway?" Nat demanded.

"Looking for a damn rustler we were!"

"I'd like to press charges too," Slocum said, keeping Dunny broadside to them.

"What's your name?" the sheriff asked, narrowing his eyelids as he studied him.

"John Slocum. That man there, a woman, and four of his rannies assaulted me without cause three weeks ago when I was coming up here."

"You will have to come to Buffalo and sign a paper."

"I will do that."

"You're not going to believe that lying damn rebel trash, are you?" McEntosh demanded.

"He's got every right to swear out a warrant as you do, McEntosh."

"It's a bloody poor day on the Powder River when scum like those two can twist the law to their own benefit." The foreman's hand went to his gun butt.

"Sit tight," Slocum said, ready to solve the Scotsman's complaint's with a .44 slug. "Or you'll be poking up daisies, big man. I ain't forgot the beating you gave me, and if you want to be the first face-down off his horse here, then you make one more move for that Colt of yours."

"Everyone get off them gun handles!" the lawman demanded. "Nat, you come in and surrender when you get those ponies home. And you, mister, I don't like gun talk like that, but if you want to file a report you can do that at the courthouse." He used the saddlehorn to square himself in the saddle. "This county ain't going to be a bloodbath because some of you can't hold your tempers. McEntosh, you and your men can ride back with me or go your own way. But we ain't having no damn gunfighting in my county." He reined his horse back a few feet and waited for a reply.

"You know I'll be there as soon as I get this stock home. But it's a frame-up, Sheriff," Nat said.

"Good. You coming to press charges?" he asked Slocum.

"I'll be along too."

"You mean you aren't arresting him?" McEntosh demanded.

"Can't you see he's got his whole horse herd here and it's nigh on to roundup time?" The sheriff shook his head in disbelief. "He needs to get them ponies home so he can be ready."

"Major Walcott won't allow no rustlers riding with him," McEntosh said, and reined his horse around, motioning to his hands that he was leaving. "You can bet your wages on that!"

"Nat, stay put! They're leaving." Slocum rode in and put his arm out to hold back Nat, who looked furious enough to bite the heads off big nails.

"Did you hear that threat!" Nat demanded.

"Wasn't a threat. Sounded to me like a promise," Slocum said softly.

"Sheriff, what you going to do about that?" Nat asked, moving his horse in close with a scowl on his face. "I'll damn sure ride spring roundup and look after my interests or there will be hell to pay."

The lawman watched after them as the FXT riders raced toward the southeast. Then, clasping the saddlehorn as if in deep thought, he finally looked up mildly.

"There's clouds of war up here, Nat. I don't like it. I'm not going to choose sides. I can't. Be sure you come in and surrender."

"It's a damn lie."

"That ain't my task. I let Judge Michaels decide those things. Just come in peacefully." He nodded good day to both of them, and then reined his horse around to leave.

"I'll be there," Nat said after him.

They watched the sheriff jog his horse off through the sage, headed for town.

"Let's get these broom-tails home," Nat said, and shook his head in defeat.

9

"Why, Nat Champion, you can't surrender yourself to some rigged court," Jen said upon learning of his plans.

"Judge Michaels ain't on their payroll."

"They ain't in this not to win. They mean to get you put away and have the roundup to suit themselves. They know you're the leader of the small ranchers up here."

"Aw, I won't say that." Nat dropped his head and shook it in despair.

"Let's send for Sandy Crocker," she said, pacing back and forth. "He's the best lawyer in the territory and the only one that the small ranchers can trust. We'll have him come tell us what to do."

"Man, he'll cost a hundred bucks." Nat acted as if her notion was too costly.

"Better that than you missing roundup," Slocum said, leaning his butt on the hitch rack before the Van Doren house.

"I'm not missing roundup." Nat cut around to look

at him with a cold glare. "I never butchered no FXT calf and stuck the hide in my shed. It is all lies."

"We can raise that sum in a day for his expenses," Jen said, still talking about the lawyer. "I'll ride to Buffalo and wire Crocker to come as quick as he can."

"That would be the best thing, Nat," Slocum said. "Then let him decide about the conditions of your surrender and find out what other evidence they have."

"Them three are going to get on the stand and lie like dogs about finding that damn hide in my shed." Nat pounded his fist in his palm. "They'll do it sure as hell. They said so, didn't they, Slocum?"

"How many folks from around here would get on the stand and say they were in that shed and never saw that hide?"

"We could get a dozen or more to say the opposite that hate her and her high-handed ways," Jen said. "I'm getting Brownie saddled and riding to Buffalo to wire Crocker. Nat, you keep out of sight and I'll bring him up to your place the minute he comes."

"I hate to hide from anything or anyone."

"No problem. In a few days this matter will be all settled and you can go to the roundup a free man," she said to reassure him.

"Thanks, Jen. Well, Slocum, we better get these ponies to the house. It'll be dark by the time we get there."

"Stay here and have supper," she told them. "It's all fixed and more than Dad will eat."

"Naw, we best ride on. Thanks," Nat said as she ran off to get her saddle horse.

Slocum watched her run, enjoying the rocking gait and the view of her shapely backside. Lots of woman there. A shame his pard never saw it.

"Nice of her," Nat said, swinging in the saddle. "To do that for me."

"Yeah, it sure is. You mention to her about your

friend coming to roundup?'' Slocum asked as he mounted, then checked Dunny to stand.

"No, I've got time for that. Let's get these broom-tails home.''

"Sure thing, Boss,'' Slocum said quietly, and waved to Jen as she brought out the bay horse and prepared to saddle him. Poor Nat was between the devil and a hard rock, and getting deeper in his own quicksand by the hour. Slocum almost couldn't wait for Etta's arrival. Whew, there were sure to be fireworks like the Fourth of July in China Town when those two met. He leaned over and undid the chestnut's lead rope from the fence, and then started out down the lane with Nat chousing the rest behind him.

Nicky must have heard them coming, for he had the corral gate open and had a lantern to see by when they swept in under the stars at Nat's place.

"Howdy, Slocum, how was the ride?''

"Good for my part, but Nat can tell you the rest.''

"Was that damn Scotsman around here snooping while I was gone?'' Nat swung off his horse and rushed over to Nicky.

"There were some riders on the ridge the other morning. I got out the Winchester and aimed to part their hair, but they rode off. No, ain't been no one here but Ruff, the collie, and me. Why?''

Nat went on to explain the situation to the young hand as they unsaddled and then turned their horses in with the herd. Nicky carried the lamp to the house.

"Man, you fellows had some time getting them horses back. I've got some food left—there ain't much—but you two must be starved.''

"We're past that,'' Nate said. They reached the porch and went inside the cabin single-file.

"There's a deer carcass on the back porch. I can cut off some steaks and fry them,'' Nicky said.

"Fire up the stove," Slocum said, and clapped the young man on the shoulder. "I can eat a few and Nat can eat a half dozen."

"How come you two didn't eat with Jen?"

"Because she was in an all-fired hurry to get that lawyer Crocker up here." Nat put his rifle on top of two pegs on the wall close to the door, and then tossed his hat on a moose rack. "Good to be home, pard."

"I'd say so too," Slocum said.

"There's more vension if this ain't enough," Nicky said a few minutes later, coming in with a heaping handful of fresh red meat to fry.

"That'll do," Slocum assured him. He fished out a cigar from his vest pocket and torched it.

Nat busied himself building a fire in the round rock fireplace. The cool air was sweeping off the snowcaps, and by morning it would be cold enough to wear a mackinaw. A fire would take the chill off things.

His shoulder leaning against a large round peeled post that held the peak of the cabin's roof, Slocum drew deep and savored the pleasure of the rich smoke. Gradually, the nicotine sought his bloodstream and began to settle him from the turn of events of the day.

"Get us a shot of whiskey," Nat said, still working on the fire. "Nick, get him the bottle."

Slocum took the brown bottle from the youth, and then waited for the two tumblers. He popped the cork and poured a few fingers in each glass, waiting for Nat to join him.

"Here's to roundup!" Nat said, joining him and raising his glass.

"And Etta helping."

"Who's helping?" Nicky asked with a frown.

"An, ah, lady friend of mine from over at Story's coming to help," Nat said with a frown of disapproval for Slocum.

"I know her?"

"No, you don't. Etta Watson is her name, and don't go telling everyone you know about it!" Nat finished the whiskey in one long drink and then slammed the glass down on the table. "It ain't for public knowledge."

"Heavens, Nat, I just wondered." Nicky shrugged and busied himself cooking the meat.

"You better have some more to drink. The mood that you're in, why, you'd clabber milk before a cow could give it," Slocum said, refilling his glass.

"It ain't funny, Slocum. It's damn serious."

"It'll damn sure be that way when that dance hall girl shows up at roundup. Be funny watching you squirm your way out of it." He raised his glass to toast his friend's discomfort, and then laughed out loud. Lord, things were going to be thick as pudding before this was all over.

10

"Ned! Ned Champion!" Someone outside was shouting. The three of them came awake in the dark cabin. With only the glow of the coals in the hearth, Slocum found his vest, removed a lucifer from the pocket, and then struck it alive. Nick brought a lamp for him to light.

"Go easy," Slocum said sharply to Nat, who was already at the door. "It could be a trick."

"Who's out there?" Nat demanded, and they listened. Their shadows from the reflector and the fireplace's light danced across the walls.

"Shorty Davis!"

"Hell, what's wrong, Shorty?" Nat asked, lifting the bar.

"They stormed into the Griffin's place tonight and run off all his horse stock. They stampeded them over his oldest boy and he ain't expected to live."

"When? Nick, get our horses saddled. They hurt that boy?"

"Wait." Slocum laid a hand on his shoulder to stop him. "Nicky and I can go see about this. You wait here until that lawyer comes. They may want it to look like you took tail and run. Then you'd be a fugitive and give them a chance to gun you down to keep the law."

"You think they done this on purpose?" Nat's eye brows furrowed in concern.

"I think they very well could have. They ever run off stock before?"

"No. It could be rustlers."

"It could be lots of things. Nicky and I'll go up there and figure it out if we can. You stick close to this place until Crocker gets here."

"Crocker's coming here?" Shorty asked.

"He's supposed to," Nat said, stepping off the porch to talk to the mounted cowboy. "They've drummed up some charges about me killing an FXT calf."

"That bunch of bastards need to be taught a good lesson," Shorty said as Nick and Slocum took the lamp and hurried for their horses.

Finally saddled and mounted, they joined Shorty and prepared to leave Nat. He stood in the doorway, holding the lantern and shaking his head ruefully at his plight.

"Whatever you do," Slocum warned him before they trotted off into the night, "keep a cool head and remember that this may be their plan to get us away and try to take you on." With that, the three men rode out.

"Who's coming in?" Out of the night, someone armed with a rifle challenged them as they rode up to the Griffins' place. They'd been in the saddle for about three hard hours of riding to reach their destination. Feeling tired, Slocum hoped they could get a few hours of sleep before another day of searching began.

"Shorty, Nick Ray, and a friend called Slocum.

How's that boy that got run over in the stampede?'' Shorty asked.

"They say he won't last until the doc can get here.''

"Damn, he was a good kid.'' Shorty slumped in the saddle in disappointment. "He'd a been twelve, I think, in the summer.''

"Anyone see anything? A face or recognize them?'' Slocum asked. He turned up his collar against the cold, and was grateful for the wool coat he wore. His breath was coming in clouds of vapor in the darkness that separated them from the large fire ahead.

"Naw, they struck like lightning. Sam was gone up to his other place, and before the Missus could stop Elliot, he ran out to head off the horses and got run over,'' the guard said. "Someone's going to pay for his death. They've sent for an Injun tracker. He should be here by first light.''

"I'll bet they covered their tracks,'' Shorty said, shaking his head wearily.

"Hell, they can't hide ten horse tracks.''

"Someone send for the law?'' Slocum asked.

"What'll he do?'' the guard scoffed.

"That boy dies, it will be a case of murder.''

"Everyone figures they wanted to scatter Sam's horses so he won't have any to ride for roundup, and make it look like rustlers did it.''

"Daylight may show us more. Let's ride up and find a place to catch some sleep,'' Slocum said to Nick. Then he booted Dunny on. They could stay out there and argue all night about what to do, but he wanted some sleep.

"I just can't believe they ran them horses over that little boy doing that,'' Nicky said, as if he could not fathom the facts, and shook his head in disbelief as they rode toward the house under the stars.

"He was just a victim,'' Slocum said. "There will be

more of them, I promise you. This is only the tip end. There's lots more coming."

Introductions were made around the armed camp when they rode up and dismounted. The grim mood of the assembled men showed on their haggard faces. Every one of the ranchers around the fire in the yard carried a Winchester, Spencer, or Sharps. They were bitter men, locked in by the darkness, unable to turn their ire on the accused until the first light, when they could take up the killers' trail. Excusing themselves, Nick and Slocum found a spot under a pine tree and brought out their rolls. Shorty went off to see about the boy's condition.

It could all wait until morning as far as Slocum was concerned. Nothing he could do for the injured boy that one of the others hadn't already done. He wondered as he laid his head on the saddle how many other small outfits had had their horse stock scattered that same evening. The tragedy of the boy's injury had drawn them from their home places, and that had left many vulnerable herds.

As he settled down, he hoped his concerns were unfounded. Only dawn would answer that. Nat needed to stay where they left him. The FXT bunch needed no legal excuse to gun him down. Maybe this lawyer Crocker could straighten out Nat's legal problems. And what was this major like? Slocum still had him to meet and, as he shut his eyes, he didn't look forward to that day.

Sunup came soft as a flannel blanket. A cloud bank hid the first sight, and the gray light shown on the peaks long before the area around their bedrolls was even out of the deep darkness. Slocum rubbed his hands briskly in the chilly morning air. He put on his coat to maintain some of the body heat left from his bedroll, and slapped on his hat. He made a circuit behind the corral to empty his bladder, then went to the campfire to refill it with strong coffee.

"Did the boy make it through the night?" he asked an older man squatted on his boot heels slurping coffee beside the fire.

"Nope, died an hour ago."

"Slocum's my name."

"Jarvis Teal, nice to meetcha. You're Nat's friend, huh?"

"Yes."

"Shorty told us about you." The man rose up at the approach of a rider coming in. Barely big enough to sit in the saddle, the child could hardly be seen as he reined up.

"Erwin?" Teal shouted.

"It's me, Uncle Jarvis, that you? Maw said for Dad to come home quick. They done run off all our horses, everyone but Red here."

"Ransom! Get out there, your boy just rode in!" Jarvis shouted.

"What's going on?" A flush-faced man rushed out of the cabin to the boy, who had slipped from the saddle to look around for his father.

"Erwin, what happened?" his father asked, taking the child in his arms.

"They done run off all our horses," the boy said, hugging his parent as he knelt before him.

"Damn!" Slocum swore under his breath. It was just as he'd suspected, a plot to draw the menfolk off so they could scatter the others' stock.

"What the hell is going to happen next?" Teal asked.

"Way I figure it, they're going to move the roundup up a week," Slocum said, blowing the vapor off his coffee cup and studying the snowcaps in the sun.

"You think they'll try to do that?" Teal cocked an

eyebrow as he looked with a question at him.

"No." Slocum shook his head. "I know they'll do it. They've got Nat Champion bottled up on a phoney charge of rustling. I'd bet a sizeable sum that last night they've scattered more horse herds than these two we know about. With everyone off guard, they'll call for a roundup at their convenience and tough luck on the small outfits."

"Be some mighty upset folks," Teal said.

"They can brand what they want and how they want it. You all can't legally brand your own outside of at roundup, nor mavericks on the range, so this fall there will be lots of slick ears and they can claim all of them."

"It would ruin many of the small ranchers, barely hanging on."

"That's their purpose. I've seen this done before."

"Damn, mister, I believe you got the whole thing down to a T and doting the I."

"Slocum, here comes that Injun tracker," Nicky said, joining them.

The man rode a long-headed paint and wore an unshaped round-crown hat with eagle feathers in the band. He reined up, and several of the men joined him.

"This here is Whooping Cough," someone said, and took the Indian to the tracks.

"That's them," the man said, pointing at the prints in the dirt, and the buckskin-clad Indian dismounted and studied the various differences in the prints. He walked in circles examining the tracks. Then he gazed off to the north and nodded. In a bound, he was on his thin horse and pointed toward the way they went.

"Go ahead, Whooping Cough. We're coming. Men, get your horses."

"We going with them?" Nicky asked Slocum.

"No, I think we better double back to Nat's. There's enough guns going with them." Besides, he suspected all that the tracker and the posse probably would find were the Griffins' horses. Alone at his ranch, Nat might be in more danger than anyone else.

They saddled their horses as men rushed in haste to catch up with the tracker. Slocum tied down his bedroll as Shorty stopped beside him.

"Nice to meet you. You going back?" Shorty asked, holding up his pony, anxious to join the others leaving in a cloud of dust.

"Yes, I want to be sure they don't drygulch Nat."

"Good idea. Thanks for coming. It looks like we got crew enough to handle them."

Slocum waved as the man raced off after the others. He jerked down his stirrup and then swung up on Dunny. This whole scheme was better planned than it appeared. First, they put Nat under the threat of arrest. Then they scattered several remudas so the small outfits were on foot.

If Slocum was thinking right, Nat's ponies had not strayed as far north as Story by themselves—they'd been pushed. That was what he recalled Jen's father, Emil, had figured. The location of the remuda was planned. That way the FXT bunch knew where Nat was going when he and Slocum rode out in that direction. Then they led the sheriff up there instead of out to Nat's ranch to confront him. They hoped to have Nat arrested and the horses still loose up there, so that even if he got out of the drummed-up charges, his horses would still have to be brought back. Maybe even push them further them-selves—it made sense. Too much was adding up, though he couldn't prove it. But it fit in place too perfectly.

"Do we need to hurry?" Nicky asked, bringing Slo-cum back to the present.

"It wouldn't hurt," he said, rising in the stirrups and setting Dunny into a long trot.

The sun was near noontime overhead when they drew

close to Champion's headquarters. The sharp whang of a high-powered rifle's report carried to them as they crossed the last rise and started down the valley for Nat's. Another shot reverberated off the hills. Nicky looked puzzled, but by then Slocum had set heels to Dunny and laid the reins on the horse's neck.

"They've got Nat pinned down," he shouted to the boy.

As the powerful dun raced through the sagebrush, Slocum eased down and jerked his .44-40 Winchester from the scabbard. Levering a shell in the chamber, he urged the big horse on. He saw the puff of smoke on the hillside. The shooter had a high-powered long-range rifle, probably used a scope. It might be a buffalo gun. The report was loud enough. How many more bushwhackers were up there?

A burst of gunfire from the cabin brought a smile to his face. Nat was well enough to shoot back anyway. Slocum reined in the dun and studied the situation. He needed to ride south and circle the gunman on the hill.

"You circle in that way." He pointed to Nicky, and sent his horse off to circle around the attacker.

"Be careful," Nick shouted after him.

But there was no time to reply to the youth. Dunny was grabbing ground, darting around clumps of sage, his hooves striking the dirt and turning up clods of sod as he raced like the wind. He was a powerful horse—trot him ten miles and he could still win a race. Slocum reined him around some junipers, hoping to reach the gunman before he fled. He had lots of questions to ask that ranny. Maybe he'd let him explain himself to the sheriff, maybe about a boy's death.

Slocum reined Dunny up. A rider on a bay was streaking south. Slocum had spooked him. Damn, he had used up his own horse, and had no intention of running Dunny in the ground and ruining him. The fleeing horse and rider disappeared from his view into the junipers.

Snorting and breathing hard, the dun stepped high as Slocum held him in check and rode toward where the shooter had been. Might be something left on the ground he could use, some evidence, something more than empty cartridges.

11

"You all right?" Slocum called out as Dunny slid to a stop in front of Nat's cabin and he jumped from the stirrups.

"Aw, they scratched me," Nat said, coming out with his arm wrapped and a blood spot showing through the sheet dressing.

"Looks worse than that to me. Get inside, that back-shooter is gone. I want a gander at that arm."

"Nothing to it," Nat said, shaking his head.

"They hit you?" Nicky asked, wide-eyed, joining them.

"Ain't nothing now. Don't you two go making a fit over me."

'We will if we want," Slocum said. "Boil some water, Nick. We'll make sure he don't get an infection in it."

"It's only a scratch."

"We'll be the judge of that."

"You see the sumbitch?" Nat asked.

"No, sit down. He lit a shuck on a racehorse and Dunny was done in."

"Damn, I went for a bucket of water and he was out there. Caught me halfway to the well. The first shot spun me around and I dove on the ground. The rest were shots into the well. I managed to slither back in the house on my belly and return some lead. But it was sure a long-range rifle he had. Must have had a telescope on it. What you thinking?"

"Maybe they didn't want you dead." Slocum unwrapped the bandage.

"You think it was her?"

"Maybe. What have you got for an antiseptic?" He looked around. Nicky was busy stoking up the sheet-metal stove to heat water.

"Coal oil?"

"I've got whiskey in my saddlebags. You got any in here?"

"Sure. Nick, get him a bottle from my stock," Nat said, trying to see where the bullet had exited out the back of his arm.

The youth brought the bottle and set it down on the table. Slocum used his teeth to uncork it, and poured it on the clean bandage Nat had torn until it was soaked with the liquor.

"Here, give me a snort of that before you put that fire on my arm." Nat reached over with his good arm, hoisted the bottle by the neck, and took a deep draught. Then he shouted, "I need to drink more. Damn, Slocum. That hurts worse than the bullet did."

"You're lucky it didn't do more damage than that."

"You think she was out there?"

"She's a dead shot with some kind of rifle. I told you that I suspected she intended to only nick me and then lord it over me."

"You two talking about Imagene Furston?" Nicky asked with a frown, bringing a steam-spouting kettle from the stove. Slocum indicated for him to pour some in the basin. Then he rinsed out his cloth and went back to washing the area around the wound.

"Yes, and by Gawd, if that bitch did this—damn, that's hot enough—I'll personally whip her bare butt with a willow switch," Nat said, holding his arm up so Slocum could clean away the dirt and debris that he had picked up bellying like a crawfish to get back into the house.

"I can't prove a thing, but you know what I told you I suspected?" Slocum said.

"Damn, they killed the Griffin boy and nearly killed Nat and then lied about the rustling," Nicky lamented. "They sure don't play fair, do they?"

"No, and you haven't seen it all yet," Slocum said, washing out his cloth in the hot water, then letting it set to cool on the edge of the basin for a second so he could handle it and to do more cleaning.

Nat took another swig of the whiskey, and Slocum took a round, then handed it to Nicky. The young hand swallowed hard as he looked at the bottle as if undecided, but then he took a big snort. With a deep sound of pain from his burning throat, he handed the bottle back and blinked his eyes. They began to water.

"Tough stuff," he said, and then his Adam's apple rose and fell. He used the corner of his kerchief to mop the tears from his face, and then cleared his throat.

"They ran off several bunches of horses from others last night," Slocum informed Nat. "They used the first attack as a diversion and struck up and down the valley."

"That Elliot was only a little shaver." Nat shook his head before raising the bottle to his lips for more.

"Twelve years old."

"Last fall during roundup, he helped the cook in camp. I remember he had a little Texas pony that could turn a cow back quicker than anything I ever saw. She could face one off and keep her there. It was all he could do to ride her when she got down and *cowed*. Had she been two hands bigger, ten men would have tried to buy her at any price."

"He's made his last roundup," Slocum said, binding the upper arm tight in a fresh bandage.

"What do we do next?" Nat asked, looking over the wrapping.

"Jen, I figure, will either have the lawyer coming or bring word."

"She's overdue, isn't she?" Nat said.

"I may saddle a horse and ride that direction. Nick, keep an eye on him and I'll be back."

"I can ride a horse," Nat declared.

Slocum waved his offer away as he sliced some cheese and used some of the crackers on the table. Nat, even though he might be a target, needed to stay put.

"I told you they wanted you to run," Slocum said.

"Going looking for Jen isn't running," Nat protested.

"Stay here and heal. Besides, you drink much more of that painkiller and you'd fall out of the saddle and restart that arm bleeding."

"I'll be certain he behaves, Slocum."

"Good, Nick, you do that. I plan to be back by dark."

"I ain't a damn baby," Nat grumbled, and in disgust slammed the bottle down on the table.

"Take care of him. I'll ride one of your ponies. Dunny needs the rest."

"Frosty is a good one," Nat said after him. "And you be careful."

"I will." Slocum saluted him from the doorway, and headed for the corral.

The ride to the Van Doren place went uneventfully.

He found Emil feeding chickens grain with an apron full of cracked grain. The older man raised up and smiled.

"How's it going?" Emil asked.

"Been rough. They run off some horses, killed the Griffin boy in the stampede. Some drygulcher wounded Nat in the arm. He'll live. You seen Jen?"

"She took off in a big stir after she heard about them trying to arrest Nat on them trumped-up charges."

"She didn't come home last night?" He wondered what had delayed her.

"No, she planned to stay in town with Mrs. Hawkins if she couldn't get a hold of that lawyer fella. What else has gone wrong?" Emil frowned in disbelief at all he had told him.

"Been plenty happening the past twenty-four hours," Slocum said, slipping to his feet and then pulling his canvas pants down by the inside of the legs. He went on to tell the man about the rest.

"Mercy, that gal and her rannies are sure out to gut this country, ain't they."

"There must be more big outfits in with her. One gal and a handful of riders can't do all this."

"Did you know they've got this club in Cheyenne? Call it the Cheyenne Social Club, for cattlemen. But hell, everyone knows it ain't nothing but a high-class private whorehouse. Every big rancher in the territory belongs to it, and they go down there and dream up such things as this. Why, they've tried twice in Congress to get the Homestead Law exempted in Wyoming. Hell, if they'd had a few more Congressmen in their pockets, by damn, they'd a got it done." He shifted on his crutches and finished feeding the scratching hens, then started for the porch.

"You mean, so no one could homestead in Wyoming?" Slocum accompanied him to the house.

"Damn right, and to negate all the claims already here. Oh, they do things in a big way."

"I figure you were right about them horses of Nat's being drifted up toward Story on purpose." Slocum sat on the stoop as the older man took a seat in a rocker on the porch.

"Funny thing to me was them cow ponies always stayed close to this valley for the past three years that he's been here. What made you think it was them done it?" Emil asked.

"When the sheriff came up there to find Nat instead of coming to his ranch. McEntosh knew where Nat was going."

"What'll they do next?" The older man folded his gnarled hands in his lap and waited for the reply.

"If I knew that, I'd try to stop them. I really think they'll move roundup to next week. They've got horses scattered to hell and gone, a boy killed in the deal, and Nat wounded as well as under suspicion for rustling."

"Be about right. You got any plans?"

"Yes, I'm going to ride to Buffalo and see if the good major has arrived and what his plans are. I'll check on her too,"

"You're a drifter, Slocum. No roots, huh?"

"No roots. Take care. I'll be sure that gal of yours is safe for you."

"She won't take much looking after." He grinned and nodded. "But I thank you for looking out for her. She's sure had a case on Nat Champion ever since he came up here, and I guess he can't see her."

"Don't we all want what we can't have? See you, Emil." Slocum went and redid the cinch, then tossed the reins over the white horse's neck and bounded in the saddle. He saluted the man and rode on toward town.

With Frosty in a long trot, Slocum stood in the stirrups and headed for Buffalo. He'd never thought to ask

Emil where Mrs. Hawkins lived, but he could learn that when he reached town. His main thoughts were on the major and running up the time to start roundup. That had to be their plans when they'd begun all their skull-duggery. This Cheyenne Social Club, as Emil called it, must have some big minds in its inner circle.

"Slocum." Jen waved her hat at him as he dropped off the ridge toward the collection of buildings clustered on the creek.

Grateful to see her, he headed in her direction. She was obviously riding out of town, so perhaps she knew about the lawyer. He drew Frosty up short and sat enough sideways in the saddle to ease his stiff back while he waited.

"Crocker's coming on the stage in the morning," she said, riding up. "I've got his telegram here." She patted the pocket on her jumper and reined up her horse. "They just put up a new notice too."

"Don't tell me," Slocum said. "They're starting roundup a week early?"

"Yes, how did you know? Major Wolcott has to go to Washington to testify before Congress the end of the month and can't get out of it."

"Damn convenient. Isn't there anyone else to head the roundup?"

"I guess not. Why?"

He began to explain all that had happened. She shook her head in disapproval listening to his story. When he finished, he could see she wanted to know more about Nat's condition.

"He'll be fine if he don't get an infection in it."

"I better go up there and take care of him. Heaven knows that Nicky, why, he's just a boy and what does he know about keeping the bandage and wound clean?"

"What about Crocker?"

"I'll send Nicky in after him to meet the stage with

a buckboard. I don't even know if he rides a horse. Some of them lawyers are kind of citified even if they do represent ranchers.''

"On the way you check on Emil so he isn't worried. I came from there and he acts fine, but I don't want him fretting about you," Slocum said.

"Good idea. I'll take some things. What kind of pain is Nat in?"

"Nothing whiskey ain't cutting, so far."

She looked at the sky, and then she shifted restlessly in the saddle, ready to hurry on. He could see her impatience, and nodded good-bye.

"Ride with care. There's enough backshooters in this basin to fill a train car.''

"Slocum?" Her brown eyes meet his. "Who are you?"

"I'm the guy that most mothers warn their daughters about.''

"Damn, I like that." She winked at him and then set spurs to the bay.

"Don't kill that horse getting there, Nat Champion ain't half close to dying yet!" he shouted after her. Then he shook his head for his words had fallen on deaf ears.

For a long while, he sat Frosty and watched her churn up dust as she raced toward the valley. Nat was fixing to get a real nursemaid. He chuckled as he dismounted and searched around before he emptied his bladder. Then, feeling relieved, he swung into the saddle and rode into Buffalo.

In town, he boarded Frosty at the wagon yard, and then walked the two blocks in the town to the Hennesey Bar. Crossing the barroom through a cloud of cigar smoke, he crowded up to the bar and ordered some bonded rye. He tossed down the first double and lighted a fresh cigar he chose from the glass bottle the barkeep brought him. From across the room, she came in a dress

of lime-colored calico. Low cut, it exposed her stark
white breast tops. Her dark hair was wound up and piled
on top of her head. She stopped before him to let him
examine the merchandise. He refused her with a head
shake. Another time, another place, maybe. His decline
sent her sauntering across the room, looking for another
prospect, as he tried to make out the players in the card
game closest to the bar.

Satisfied the stakes were low enough, he waited until
one man rose and left the game. These men were not
locals; they also had money to play cards after payday.
He had seen plenty of their kind on the Texas-to-Kansas
drives. They were working on a better payroll than most
hands. Not the average cowboy anyway—they obviously worked for a big rancher.

"This seat taken?" Slocum asked, moving behind the
chair with his untouched glass of whiskey in his hand.
He introduced himself to the others, who nodded behind
their hands and gave their names one at a time.

"Dave."

"Chuck."

"Ferral."

"Devon."

"You must be new here," Dave said, dealing the
cards to the others.

"Not been here long," he said, digging out twenty
dollars in silver and stacking it, ready for the next deal.

"You looking for work?"

"Oh, I might be depending how my luck goes here."

"They're fixing to start roundup here next week,"
Dave explained, and Ferral nodded to add to the au-
thenticity of the man's statement. "We've heard that the
local ranchers have been having trouble with some of
their neighbors stealing their horses. Some of them
might not be able to go on the drive. Major Wolcott is
due in here on the stage Friday, and if them damn squat-

ters can't ride out, he may take on some hands."

"You work for him?" Slocum looked mildly at them, waiting for an answer, as Devon raked in a pot.

"Me and Ferral do," Dave said. "We brought up his private wagon and horses so they'd be ready for him."

"I guess a man like the major has lots of things, personal gear, to take out on roundups." Slocum anted a dime with the others, waited for the deal, then picked up his cards and fanned them carefully. Two queens were all he had worth saving. "I worked for an outfit where the boss man had his own brand of canned tomatoes."

"Bid fity cents," Chuck said.

"Hell, all out of the ordinary that old man takes is his own whiskey," Dave said. "He drinks expensive stuff. I've got it under lock and key. Farnsworth is the brand. Made in New York somewhere."

Slocum covered the bet. His next problem was where they stashed the liquor. If he knew that he could proceed.

"I'll raise it a quarter," Ferral said, and tried to conceal a big smile.

Slocum saw the bet and the raise, then discarded three cards for new ones. He drew three more small cards, and after both Chuck and Ferral drew two cards each, he folded his hand. Chances were good they each had three of a kind.

"Beat three nines," Chuck said, proudly laying out his hand.

"Beat three queens," Ferral said.

Slocum considered the winning hand and tossed his cards in face-down. Damn new kind of game—this deck had five ladies in it. Fine, he could see how there might be five of a kind even without a wild card in such a deal.

"I guess it ain't my night to win, count me out," he said, and then he downed his drink.

"Stick around," Dave said. "Your luck may change."

"No, I lose this stake, I might end up cleaning outhouses. Say, I may come see you about that job. Where are you at?"

"The wagon yard. I've got his rig and his horses ready for the major. Fussy old bastard, but he pays good."

"I'd bet he does. See you," he said, and rose. He pocketed his money, save a dollar, and when he started to leave, the same girl moved in place to block his exit. Obviously she had not found any takers so far. He stopped, then reached over and carefully shoved the silver cartwheel down between her firm breasts. With a wink and smile, he drew his hand out.

"Hey, you ain't such a bad sport after all," she said. Then she fished it out from between her breasts. Deliberately, she reset the right brown nipple back out of sight and straightened her dress front. "You've got credit with me."

"Yes, ma'am," he said, and touched his hat brim for her and left the saloon.

He found the diner down the street and ordered a steak and potatoes. The waitress brought him coffee and went on her way. With his back to the wall, he could see the front door, and watched as two of the FXT hands came in and took their place at the counter. The same two had ridden with McEntosh when they'd tried to have Nat arrested and the sheriff had spoiled their plans.

If they saw him sitting there, he couldn't be certain. Nothing in their facial expression or actions had given it away. But in case they had any stupid ideas, he undid the thong on the hammer of the Colt in his holster. He decided they had been drinking, and so maybe had not noticed him. Good.

The waitress brought his meal and asked if he needed

anything else. He gave her a head shake and started in on his plate of food, savoring each bite and considered his next move.

Before he could even consider his plan, he needed to find a slippery elm tree. Was there such a plant in the basin? He planned to make some slippery elm bark tea to lace the major's private whiskey with. If Major Wolcott couldn't get away from the outhouse, the roundup might be put off long enough to let the settlers gather their loose horses.

He needed some help to do all this. Nicky would help him, but who else? Jen? He probably couldn't pry her from poor wounded Nat's side. Who could he get to help? No one came to mind. Maybe he and the boy could do it. They would need an opportunity to add the tea to the liquor.

Come daylight, he would look up this Mrs. Hawkins. Since she put up with a tomboy like Jen, she might be the right person to help. He hoped so. The nearest thing to a dose of castor oil he could think of was this old Indian remedy for constipation. There was very little taste to slippery elm bark tea, especially in whiskey. The major would never detect it, but he might need a powder puff for his ass before it was over.

12

"Yes, there's some elms down in that meadow," Emil said as he stood on his crutches.

"Thanks," Slocum said. "I guess Jen's gone to nurse Nat back to health?"

"Oh, yes, and I suppose I'll be batching by myself for a while with roundup due to start next week, they say. She'll be off on that next."

"You heard anything about those horses they scattered the other night?" Slocum asked, knowing that various ranchers had been by the place to talk with the man.

"Couple ranchers came by this morning and said they're all over. They scattered them good."

"I guess, if we had a week or so longer, they could gather the most of them."

"Yes, but—"

"Don't make any promises, but if my plan works, they'll have extra time to find those ponies."

"I won't ask how." Emil smiled and shook his head

in amusement. "I think if you had some help you could outfox the whole damn Cheyenne Social Club."

"For a day or two, maybe. Say, I need to borrow your ax."

"Help yourself, it's around at the wood pile."

"I'll need a sack or two from the barn."

"Get what you need. Wish I was a whole man, I'd help you."

"When I come back, tell me about that Mrs. Hawkins." He set out in a run for the back of the house to get the hand ax. He'd use it to peel off the bark to make his medicine for the major.

"What do you need to know about that old heifer?" Emil called to him.

"I need someone I can trust. Part of my plan is to make Major Wolcott sick enough that he can't start the roundup on time. Not kill him, mind you, but I have to find a place in town to doctor two cases of good whiskey."

"Whew," Emil whistled through his front teeth. "You tell Sadie straight out your needs and purpose. If anyone will help you, she will."

"Good," Slocum said, stashing the ax in his saddlebags. The short handle protruded, but it would ride in there. "I'm going to get Nicky to help me pull this off. I figure Jen can take care of Nat."

"Good luck. Even a few more days would help them get more of their saddle stock gathered. This is Thursday, isn't it?"

"Yes, and this day is almost gone. Be careful, Emil."

"Don't worry about me none. I've been around for over seventy winters and I have a few more left in me."

Slocum hoped that the man was correct about his predictions. He had begun to take a real liking to Emil. This high-handed outfit they were up against wasn't choosy who they ran over, including young boys. An old man's life wouldn't even twinge their conscience if they thought they would gain by taking it.

It was dark by the time he reached Nat's place. He put Frosty up, and Nicky came out to talk with him.

"She's about got supper on and we have plenty. What did you learn?"

"Roundup's going to start Monday unless we can stop it."

"How can we stop it?" the boy asked.

"We need to ride for Buffalo tonight and get some things done there."

"What about this lawyer that's coming?"

"Jen's got to go meet the lawyer. You and I have got some important business to take care of in town. Nat's all right, isn't he?"

"Fine. He kinda took a turn for the worst when she came by all upset about him being shot is all."

Slocum almost laughed aloud as he washed his hands and face at the pitcher on the dark back porch. He dried himself on the towel, and slung it back on the rack. Nick was learning.

"Slocum's here," Nicky announced when they pushed inside.

"What do you know?" Nat asked, bolting up on the bottom bunk. His left arm was in a sling and he looked a little pale, but not in fever or weak from losing blood.

"I need Nicky to ride back with me and help on a deal and maybe we can postpone the roundup till midweek."

"How in the hell you going to do that?" Nat blinked at him as Jen came over from her cooking to listen.

"I figure to boil down some slippery elm bark tea. I'm going to add that to the major's expensive whiskey, and I don't think that he'll be fit to leave the crapper. Excuse me, Jen, but I think the major will have the worst case of dysentery he's ever had, even in the military."

"Where's his whiskey supply?" Nat asked.

"In the Buffalo wagon yard. He wasn't there yet, but his rannies had brought up his wagon, and the special whiskey he drinks is stored on it."

"Damn, this is exciting. Won't he figure it out?" Jen asked.

"Would if he could taste it." Slocum winked at her.

"But how are we going to get it in the whiskey?"

"I'm going to try to enlist Mrs. Hawkins to help us. Then I'm going to engage the major's men in a hot card game while Nicky makes the switch."

"Nat, will you be all right by yourself here?" Jen asked.

"Hell, I'm going and help you. Even one-armed, I can help some. What do we need?"

"How far is it from the wagon yard to Mrs. Hawkins's?" Slocum asked.

"Maybe two blocks."

"Too far. We need to make the brew, carry it down there in something, pour out about two jiggers of whiskey from each bottle, add that much elm bark tea to each bottle, and recork them. We don't know which one he'll start drinking on."

"What will we need, some gallon jugs of this tea?"

"That much anyhow."

"Oh damn, I've burned the biscuits," she shouted, and ran to rescue them from the smoking oven. In a fury she dragged out the tin of overbaked bread.

"Hell, it won't hurt them none," Slocum said. "Everyone's so fired up about this deal, they won't mind a little brown on them."

"Brown? They look charred on top to me," she said, disappointed.

He reached over and took one, quickly dropping it on the dry sink as the heat found his fingers. With his jackknife, Slocum sliced off the crust, and the steaming white center brought a smile to Jen's face.

"See, it never hurt a thing." Gingerly, he picked it up, blew hard, then bit a chunk out as if testing it. "Tastes great. Let's eat. We got miles to cover tonight."

"Do you think Nat should go?" she asked, dishing out potatoes and meat on tin plates for them as if they were starved harvest hands.

"I'd hate to try and keep him here," Slocum said, holding a full dish in each hand. "Beside, we go in late tonight no one will recognize him. We can get him out later the same way."

"Damn, I knew sending for you was a good idea. Didn't I tell you that, Nick?" Nat asked.

"You sure did. The food looks great, Jen," Nicky said as Slocum slid their heaping plates at them.

"Thanks, Nick," she said, bringing the coffeepot to the table.

Slocum watched her pause beside Nat to fill his cup. But he was busy feeding his face, and never looked up until she bumped him with a hip.

"Oh," he said, and blinked at her, and then dragged the mug to the side for her. "Slocum," Nat said, pointing his fork at him. "We can hold off that major for a few days and everyone will have their horses back. Their plan won't work."

"We're riding on the coattails of this lawyer coming to Buffalo tomorrow, right?"

"He's suppose to be coming then," Jen said, finally taking a place at the end of the table, but looking ready to jump up in case anyone needed anything.

"You learn anything else in town?" Nat asked, wiping his mouth on the back of his hand.

"Sure is good food," Nicky said again.

"Food's food," Nat said, annoyed. "Slocum, what else did you figure out?"

"I never ate none of your food that tasted this good," Slocum said.

"Dammit, it's all right!"

"It's good, admit it," Slocum said pointedly.

"That hardhead don't have to admit anything to me!" Jen said as she rose. Then she bolted from the table and out the door.

"What's wrong with her?" Nat asked.

"Stay here, I'll go find out," Slocum said, and stood up to go see about her.

"Nicky, get me some more food on this plate," Nat said behind him.

Slocum found her with her face buried in her hands at the corral in the starlight. He went up and hugged her shoulders to his chest. He gazed off at the snowy tops of the Bighorns for strength.

"Some men ain't worth worrying about," he said softly.

"I shouldn't let him get to me," she sniffed, and then wiped her face on the bandanna he swept loose from his neck for her.

"Nat can't help it. He's like a bulldog fighting a bear and he's not sure how to not be consumed by it."

"Bullheaded is a better term. I should have known by now that I don't exist as a woman for Nat Champion." She crowded inside Slocum's hug.

"I love him like a younger brother, but I could boot him hard if it would help," Slocum offered.

"It won't help." She straightened her backbone and moved his arms apart, holding his forearms as she looked up. "I don't intend to hang on to him a minute longer."

"Sounds sensible. Now let's get something to eat and we'll be ready to ride."

"No, you go back inside and do that. I'll saddle some horses. I couldn't eat anyhow. Not now." She handed back his wadded-up neckerchief and turned on her heels. He watched her in the pearly light as she walked to the shed for the saddle.

There was no way to talk her into staying there out of harm's way. He went back inside and sat down to his plate. Nicky heated up his coffee with some fresh-brewed coffee, and never said a word. The silence in the cabin was obvious.

"Did you learn anything else in town?" Nat asked, shoving his empty plate on the table to make room for his good elbow.

"They were expecting to hire some men to help the major since the ranchers had all their horses stolen and couldn't come."

"Those rotten bastards!" Nat slammed his good fist on the table, sending the plate skittering off the tabletop. It sloshed coffee out of their cups as Nat bolted up, his face black with rage.

"They want you that angry," Slocum said mildly, between bites of his food.

"I can't help it. You aren't in a sling and don't have a warrant sworn out for you—sorry, Slocum." Nat sank back into the chair and slouched down, moving the sling in front. "I guess you're right. They would like me angry enough to do something rash."

"Exactly."

"What's next?"

"Get us enough slippery elm bark to make that tea strong."

"I won't be much help."

"You can be the lookout."

"Sure," Nat agreed in defeat.

13

"We don't want all the lights turned on," Jen said to the woman in the kitchen.

In her nightcap, Mrs. Hawkins stood before them, dressed in her full-length flannel nightclothes, holding a single candle lamp. Slocum felt her dark eyes look his frame over as she appraised the two intruders in her kitchen.

"This is Slocum, and Nat and Nick Ray are outside," Jen said, as if expecting the older woman to say something.

"Tell them to come in and wipe their feet before they do."

"We need to quickly make some tea in your kitchen," Jen explained as Slocum went outside.

"Tea, at this hour?"

"A special kind, and we need to make a lot of it. I can explain it all to you. Trust me," Jen said.

"What kind of tea?"

"Slippery elm bark," Slocum said, returning with the other two.

"My goodness, are you going to purge an elephant?" she asked, lighting another lamp.

"A big one," Slocum said, and chuckled.

"I guess—my goodness, Nat Champion, whatever happened to your arm?" Mrs. Hawkins asked, discovering his sling.

"A bushwhacker grazed it."

"I must say, this country becomes more uncivilized by the day. Is it healing properly?"

"Oh, yes, ma'am."

"You all sit and I'll find the rest of you some kettles. A lot of elm bark tea. I must say, I hope it isn't used on the entire population." She busied herself handing Jen a large kettle and a big pan from the confines of her cabinets.

"Nicky, you split stove wood," Slocum said. "We're going to need plenty."

"Will you need a lamp?" Mrs. Hawkins asked, turning around from her search.

"Naw, there's enough moonlight," Nicky said.

"Don't you chop your hand, young man. One injured man on that ranch is enough."

"Oh, I'll be careful," Nicky said, and slipped outside.

"Here, you can draw some water." Mrs. Hawkins shoved a pail at Slocum. "Child, I guess the rest of my pans are small ones," she said to Jen.

"That's fine. They will work, Sadie."

Slocum found the well and drew up a bucket hand-over-hand to transfer the water to his container. From the side of the ghostly white house he could hear the soft chop of Nicky's ax. He hoped they wouldn't wake up everyone in the neighborhood with their activities. They should have the tea made by morning and ready to doctor the major's whiskey. Then he needed to get those two rannies in a card game. That shouldn't prove too hard. The big thing was when would the major arrive. Slocum glanced at the half-moon. They would need to hurry. His plan had to work—short of holding the man captive, this was the best way to stall him and fewer folks would get hurt.

"What about the guy at the wagon yard?" Slocum asked Nat as he came in with the water.

"Joe Langley?"

"I don't know him," Slocum said, pouring the water into the assembled containers on the stove top under Mrs. Hawkins's directions.

"I think I can get him drunk enough that he won't notice what we're doing," Nat offered.

"You'll have to keep out of sight. McEntosh and his bunch may show up any time." Everything full of water, Slocum backed up.

"I know and I can do that in his back room. He isn't a bad guy, but I don't know if he can be trusted entirely."

"Don't forget that Crocker is coming today," Jen reminded them as she stoked up the firebox.

"These chucks of bark need to be whittled down smaller to work better," Mrs. Hawkins said, looking at the pile of strips dumped on her square table. "Get over here and help me."

Slocum shared a wink with Jen, and then went to help the woman. He wouldn't lack for bossing around. He looked up as Nicky came in with an armload of kindling. He deposited it in the wood box and straightened.

"You can help us too," she announced to Nicky. "If Nat had two good hands we'd use him too."

Jen joined them, taking a seat beside Slocum, and soon, with their jackknifes shredding the bark, the shavings flew. The water finally boiled, and Mrs. Hawkins began adding the elm slivers.

"I have a few skeleton keys in my saddlebags," Slocum said to Nat. "One of them better open the locked chest in the major's wagon or we're up a creek without a paddle."

"I'll go get them," the youth said, and left them.

"We have all our horses in your small barn," Slocum explained.

"Won't hurt a thing. My Henry always kept more horses in there than the dang thing was made for."

"She lost him two years ago," Jen said to Slocum.

"We came up here to ranch, but Henry was past sixty and he didn't need to do that. Besides, the cold was hard on him in the winter and he didn't need to get out in it. So he traded horses and fixed saddles. Did very well."

"I can see that," Slocum said, looking around the large kitchen.

"Oh, he made his money trailing cattle to Kansas."

"Sorry that I never meet him, but there were lots of us on those trails."

"He'd been alive, why, he'd been all heated up to do this to that pompous old major. I saw that Wolcott swaggering around Buffalo last fall like he was some kind of big potentate."

The sun came up, and they were bottling the amber-colored tea in gallon crock jugs. With his finger, Slocum sampled each batch, satisfied the mild-tasting concoction was strong enough to flush the bowels of anyone who took it. Best of all, the man would never suspect it was in the whiskey.

"How are we going to get this stuff to the wagon yard?" Nicky asked, looking very tired. They'd sent Nat to bed because he couldn't hold his head up.

"I have a wheelbarrow," Mrs. Hawkins offered.

"Getting light. We better move it close and stash it near the wagon yard," Nicky said.

"Good idea," Slocum said. "We can all sleep for a day when we get it done."

"I have extra beds upstairs." Mrs. Hawkins raised her head to indicate them as she corked the next bottle.

"We'll use them later on," Slocum promised her.

His eyes felt like burned-out ash holes, and despite the hardy breakfast she cooked for them and her strong coffee, he still felt numb from a lack of sleep. But there was no time for self-pity. Nicky had the special keys, and they'd awakened Nat, so Slocum saddled Dunny and set out to find the major's men, Dave and Ferral. It was up to him to decoy the pair away from the major's wagon long enough for the others to fix the whiskey. Heaven help them.

Slocum arrived at the wagon yard, and a tall burly man came out and nodded, then stretched with a yawn.

"Morning. You leaving that hoss here?"

"I planned to," Slocum said. "Say, are the major's men here, Dave and Ferral?"

"Naw, they must be on a real bender. They never came back last night."

"Sounds like them," Slocum said, and undid the cinch. Where would they be at? Damn, this might put a crimp in their plans. He could hardly go back and stop the tea from coming, and those two rannies might stumble back any minute. Undecided, he looked up the shadowy street and saw nothing. His stomach began to churn sourly as he considered how much of his plan depended on him occupying the rannies while the switch was made.

He entered Hennesey's. One wagon wheel of lamps remained lighted overhead. A few men in suits seated at the first table looked him over mildly, and then resumed their own conversations. The sour smell of whiskey and stale cigar smoke burned his nostrils as he reached the bar.

"Morning," the thin-faced barkeep said, coming with a rag to wipe the bar top with.

"Ah, there she is," Slocum said, seeing the silver-dollar girl bring a tray of food to the men at the first table. She gave him a warm smile and an I'll-be-with-you-in-a-minute wink.

"Bring me a whiskey, good stuff," he told the barkeep as he turned back. "And one for her."

"Four bits," the bartender said, reaching for two jiggers and setting them on the bar. Then he produced a bottle and filled the glasses, looking hard at Slocum to see if he was satisfied. With a sharp nod of approval, Slocum slapped the money on the bar for the drinks.

"What can I do for you this morning?" the girl asked, holding the tray under her arm.

"Got time for a quick drink?"

"Sure." She still looked up at him, questioning his intentions, as he carried their drinks to the side table.

"My name's Rose," she said, setting the tray to the side and then using both hands to get her skirt and petticoats under her to sit down.

"Slocum's mine. Are Dave and Ferral still upstairs?"
She frowned at him.

"Those two card cheats who work for the major?"

"Those two—oh, I know who you mean. I guess so. I can go up and check on them." She started to stand up, but his hand on her forearm sat her back down. "They went up there last night," she said, and glanced at the empty staircase. "I never saw them come down this morning."

"Good, they must still be up there. I haven't got much time to explain, but for twenty dollars can you be certain they don't leave here for another hour if they do wake up?" He hoped that was enough time for his crew to make the switch. "You serve them a big free breakfast, buy them plenty of whiskey." He looked at the schoolhouse clock on the wall—6:10. They should be adding the stuff to the major's stock soon. An hour or more should be enough time if one of his keys worked on the lock.

"They won't come back at me?" She made a small frown of concern with her thin brows.

"No. You can tell them some big rancher wanted them really satisfied since they had so much work to do. You didn't know him."

He slide two ten-dollar gold pieces across the table to her. They were under his fingertips as she looked at them, then up at him.

"Lordy," she said in a whisper. "For that much I can keep them here until Hell freezes over." She rose up, then turned her face to get under his hat brim and kissed him hard on the mouth. "Come back, Slocum. For this much, why I'll give you a turn in the hay like you never had before."

"Good, I may do that. Don't be stingy with it if they come down."

"I won't," she said softly, looking with glazed eyes at him.

He left Hennesey's and hurried up the street, finding a place in front of a small residence where he could stand with his back to a tree to see Dave and Ferral coming and still view the wagon yard. With a branch to whittle on, he notched the pitchy wood with his knife.

Time passed slowly as blue jays in the tree scolded him. Some noisy schoolchildren went past and looked at him with a questioning look, then rushed on their way. Then he heard the iron wheel, and looked up the street to see Nicky pushing the barrow and heading south toward Mrs. Hawkins's. Shortly a rider went out the back way. He recognized Nat's form as he headed back to his ranch. Slocum fished a cigar out of his pocket and struck the lucifer on his pants leg. As he drew up the smoke, he saw through the haze as Jen crossed the street and headed for Mrs. Hawkins's too.

He inhaled deep, and then blew a steady stream out of his lips. Tired and sore, he dreamed of sleeping away the day. Dave and Ferral must be enjoying that special meal, for they still hadn't appeared outside the saloon. It might have been a waste of twenty bucks, but he had hired a loyal one in Rose. He never knew when he would need an ally.

Then he started for the window's house and some sleep—he hoped.

14

"Slocum, is that you?" Nicky asked in the pre-dawn light.

He rose in his bedroll to see the youth and Shorty looking at him in the early morning light. "Yes, it's me. Hello, Shorty."

"Say, we've got thirty riders coming to take Nat in," Nicky said, undoing his cinch. "That ought to be enough to insure his safety."

"Sounds good."

"You sleeping out here?" Nicky asked, glancing uneasily at Nat's cabin.

"Three makes a crowd," Slocum grinned at the boy as he pulled on his boots while seated on the blankets. "Etta is inside."

"Where did she come from?"

"She works up at Story."

"Is she going on roundup with us?" Nicky asked.

"I guess." Slocum shrugged. He rose and knifed in his shirttail with his palms.

"What are we going to do about breakfast?" Nicky asked quietly.

"Why, go up there bang on the damn door and barge in."

"You go first. Me and Shorty are right behind you."

"Yeah," Shorty agreed, acting subdued.

"Come on, boys," Slocum said, leading them across the yard, buckling on his gunbelt, and then setting his hat square. He took the pitcher and bowl on the back porch and clanged them like a dinner bell.

"Damn, Nat, we need some water to wash up with!" he said, loud enough to wake the dead.

"I'll go get some," Nicky said.

"Good. Shorty, how's the ranchers' horse-gathering getting along?"

"We'll have enough to start tomorrow. Some folks are lending their mounts so those folks in the south end can start rounding up tomorrow. Then we have a bunch of young boys out getting the rest gathered in."

"What'll you bet they don't start tomorrow?" Slocum asked.

"That damn major starts whether folks are ready or not, and he is supposed to begin in the south end in the morning."

"He might and he might not."

Shorty perked up at the notion of a delay. "Give us a week and we'll have all the strays in."

"We'll see," Slocum said as Nicky brought the water pail and filled the pitcher and bowl. He washed his hands and face, then winked at the youth, who still looked undecided about the entire thing. Slocum rapped twice at the cabin door, and then jerked the latchstring.

Nat was fighting with getting his pants up one-handed, and Etta was helping him get his galluses up.

"Morning," Nat offered as she finished.

"What are you two feeding us for breakfast?" Slocum asked, motioning to the others.

"Someone start that stove. I'll make the biscuits," Etta said, smiling at Nicky and Shorty. It was enough to give both of them red faces.

"Nicky, fix the fire for her," Nat said.

"I'll fill that water pail, ma'am," Shorty said, taking it as if any excuse to get away was all he wanted.

Slocum had to agree. Something about her made his lower flanks respond. She was a gawdawful lot of temptation to look at, poured into her tight dress, every step she made making it harder not to get notions. He could hardly blame anyone from stampeding at the sight.

The coffee finally boiled and, with the smell of her biscuits browning, deer steaks sizzled in the pan, along with a heaping skillet of potatoes. She poured them a round of coffee, then set the pot back and fiddled with her food, finally removing the two pans of biscuits from the oven. They looked perfect, and Nat fished the first one out with his fork. He spread it on his plate, grinning at her.

"Damn, darling, I believe this is the best biscuit I ever ate." he said, taking a nibble of it. "Yes, a perfect piece of bread, I must say. Where did you learn how to do this?"

"My momma taught me growing up."

"She sure did it right. Wow, boys, don't eat over two of them. The rest are mine."

Etta served them the potatoes in the skillet, and then let them choose steaks from the skillet she held with a hot-holder with both hands as she went around the table.

"Honey, you sure are a helluva cook," Nat said, hugging her hip up against him.

"Be careful, this skillet is hot," she warned.

"Why, darling, you have made the best breakfast I've had in ages. Huh, Nicky?"

"Oh, yes."

"Oh, yes? Thunder, why, we've been eating our own old sorry cooking up here too long. My, these potatoes taste like they have honey on them."

"You know how to butter a gal up," she said, standing beside him and spreading some butter on his biscuits for him. "You need me to cut that steak for you?"

"Why, I sure do, darling. You can do that for me," he said to her. "What time are them neighbors coming to ride to town today?" he finally asked Nicky.

"About eleven. I told them we needed to be in Buffalo between two and three in the afternoon."

"Good." Nat grinned up at her as she finished slicing up his meat. "I don't know how a one-armed man got along without you, darling."

"I'll be here until it's healed too." She pushed the stray wave of hair back from his forehead and then kissed him on the mouth.

"Good."

Slocum looked at the other two, busy eating and trying to ignore the whole exhibition. Poor cowboys, they were in for a lot of hell before this was over. He almost wished he would be there when she met Jenny. He closed his eyes, and then had to suppress a chuckle imagining the fit that meeting would bring on. He looked across at Nat, busy talking to Etta in his sweetest tone. You may have more than a scratched arm when this is over, he thought.

"You going to join us at roundup?" Nat asked Slocum.

"Yes, I guess I'll see the dust wherever you start down there."

"Sure thing. You be careful today."

"I will. Thanks, Etta, it was a good meal." Slocum

excused himself, and had Dunny saddled before Nicky came to the corral to talk to him.

"I guess it's all off between him and Jenny, ain't it?" the youth asked.

"You like Jen, don't you?" Slocum said, jerking down his stirrup and prepared to pull out.

"Sort of."

"Well, I think she's a fine lady and Nat is making a mistake, but it's his pickle. Isn't it?"

"Oh, Etta is fine, but she couldn't ride or rope with Jenny."

"Right," Slocum agreed. "Men are stupid at times when it comes to choosing women. They can't see what their friends can see looking in. Can they?"

"Nat sure can't."

"Nicky, keep you eyes open for what they will try next. Our plan works, we should have a half week until roundup starts."

"I'll watch out. You be careful too." The youth waved good-bye, and the others came out and did the same.

Slocum pushed Dunny, keeping to the hills so his destination would not draw witnesses. He reined up in a grove of jack pines and studied the FXT outfit in his glass. McEntosh and several hands were mounting up in front of the corrals. There was no sign of the girl as the warm morning sun heated up. Carefully, Slocum eased back, mounted up, and angled back more until he came to the gate and cross beam with the brand on a board hanging down from it.

After going through it, he kept under the brink of the hill until he was satisfied that he was far enough to dare take a peek. Settled on his belly, he could see the small stream that fed out of the mountains. The large log house, barns, low bunkhouses, pens, and blacksmith shop were scattered beyond, surrounded by the green patches of alfalfa. Then he caught sight of her black hat, and concentrated as she mounted a horse to match the silk blouse. He lost her. Then she reappeared on the dancing black headed into the mountains.

Good. He'd see where she went. He eased back to Dunny and moved higher up the hills, keeping from exposing himself to her side of the hill. He paused, climbed the rim, and tried to find her, but the sparkle of the midday sun on the brook was all he found. He remounted Dunny and rode higher.

The next time, he dismounted and climbed to the hogback, and could hear water crashing. He picked up the waterfall in his glass. It was a tall one. His eye followed it down until a flash of white caught his eye. There she stood, naked as Eve. Not realizing she was in his eyepiece, she waded out, pointed her arms, dove forward in a splash, and swam out into the pool. He lost her from view in the pine boughs that blocked his view. For a long moment, he recalled the familiar firm halves of her butt that he had seen in the glass.

Indian-like, he worked his way down the hillside, keeping to the cover as much as possible. The rush of the waterfall would hide any sound of his approach. Obviously she did not expect to be bothered by anyone, with her crew heading to roundup and her alone up here in paradise.

Finally, he strode over to where her handgun was piled on top of her clothing, and stood with his hands on his hips waiting for her to look up. She came up sputtering water, and then blinked in disbelief, holding her arms folded over her bare breasts. The nipples were knotted hard from the cold water, and drops of water slid from her like diamonds in the bright sun.

"What are you doing here?" she demanded, and tried to look past him as if someone would be coming to her rescue.

"They have all rode off to roundup," he said.

"So? What do you want?" Some of her bravado had dissolved in the face of her predicament.

"Some answers."

"To what?" She backed a step deeper into the water so that her dimpled navel was at the water's surface.

"Who killed that Griffin boy?"

"What boy?"

"The Griffin boy was run over and killed by some horse-scattering rannies three nights ago."

"I don't know what you're talking about."

He undid his gunbelt and let it drop, not taking his gaze from hers. She looked even shorter than the last time they met. Her lower lip appeared fuller than the last time as she hugged herself and tried to look around him for a way out.

His shirt vest and hat off, he slipped off his right boot standing, then toed off his left one. His socks were stripped away and thrown by his boots. Then he started into the water in his britches.

"Damn you, Slocum!" She started to wade to the side, but he easily blocked her retreat, and soon they were only feet apart.

Her eyes set on fire, she began to beat him on the chest with her fists. He encircled her with his arms as if her blows were mere taps. Then he drew her up in his hug until she was forced to raise her arms to save them from being pinned.

"You're hurting me—" His mouth sought hers. Her lips, hard as granite, soon melted and her arms flew around his neck. With her cold small breasts pressed against his chest, he lifted her higher to straighten his neck as they sought each other's tongues. Her hard-muscled thighs were in his grip to hold her up, and the fury of their passion set him on fire in the blinding sunlight reflecting off the water.

He carried her to the bank in his arms. Then he set her down. She reached for a blanket. Quickly, she spread it on the ground, then turned to him.

"No rocks and grass this time, please," she said, undoing the top button of his canvas pants.

"None," he promised, and pushed his pants off his hips.

They melted into one on top of the soft wool blanket, and soon were kissing in a fury that matched a fire in dead pine boughs. His hands were cupping her breasts, and he was smoothing her hard belly with his palm, then rubbing her mound, and then slipping in the gulf between her smooth raised legs. A silky wetness met his exploration, and she moaned as he played her taut pointed instrument like a fiddle.

Then he was over her, lowering himself between her limbs, and then thrusting inside until she was short of breath and crying in abandoned pleasure. Their fury grew faster and more intense, until the explosion left both of them sweaty and spent in each other's arms.

He moved beside her and onto his elbows, listened to the waterfall splash into the pool. She finally stretched on her back, and with effort rolled over to be beside him.

"Did you shoot Nat?" he asked, looking off at the mountains.

"No."

She was lying to save herself. How would he get the damn truth from her? There had to be a way to do it. He was too involved with her small rock-hard body to sort things out. Somewhere there had to be a way to get the facts from her. Then she draped her arm over him and pushed a knotted nipple into his chest as she clung to him.

"Go to work for me. Please?"

15

"I swear, Slocum, I never sent any of my men to scatter those horses. I never heard about the Griffin boy being trampled to death," she said over the crash of the falls beyond the pool. Naked as newborns, they sat up and faced each other. A cool wind swept over him as he considered her words.

"You shot at me." He narrowed his eyes, staring at her creamy skin.

"I never denied that. But I never shot at Nat Champion." She shook her head in defiance; her hair, out of the roll, spilled over her bare shoulders.

"Who else can skin a cat with a telescope on a needle gun?"

"I don't know." She stuck out her lower lip further.

"One of your gunhands. Which one?"

"Slocum, you've got to believe me. Those small ranchers are rustling my cattle. But I haven't ordered any of the things you are talking about.'' Her lips re-formed in a determined set for him.

"Rustling goes on everywhere. That don't mean every small rancher is stealing from you. There's lot's of God-fearing folks out there that only want what's theirs.'' Why couldn't she understand such a simple thing?

"Dammit, they are rustling hundreds of my cattle and other big outfits' stock.''

"They're people,'' he said, and then grabbed her by the shoulders and shook her hard enough to try to break her stubbornness. He finally stopped. No use hurting her, it wouldn't change her thinking. He released her and dropped his chin in defeat. "Can't you tell the differ-ence? Dammit, there's a big difference between folks seeking out a living and real crooks.''

"I can't see it. I think they're all in cahoots,'' she said, as defiant as before. Clutching her arms around her breasts, she shuddered as she drew in her breath.

"You need to put this on,'' he said, handing her his shirt as the gooseflesh covered the backs of her arms and she shivered, hugging them.

"Thanks,'' she said demurely.

"Dammit, then your Cheyenne friends sent those horse drivers,'' he declared.

"I never knew a thing about it. Don't you believe me?''

"Whose idea was moving the roundup up a week early then?'' He ignored answering her question, not sat-isfied with her denial.

"I don't know,'' she said, growing perturbed with him. "They said that the major has to be in Washington, D.C., and testify in three weeks before Congress.''

"Damn convenient that the horses on those ranches were scattered and Nat arrested at the same time that the roundup was pushed up.''

"I'm not surprised those rustlers are stealing the

smaller ones' horses is all,'' she said, shivering under the shirt she held together in the front to hide her nakedness. "My foreman swears that he found that hide in Champion's shed."

He gave her a wry look. She was freezing to death and wasn't giving him what he wanted. If she didn't know anything about anything, then someone else was calling the shots, and that would have to be another big rancher or this Major Wolcott. She had to be lying. She looked pathetic as hell, on her knees before him, quaking like the aspens did in the high country each fall. Damn mess. He took her in his arms and held her shivering form to his chest.

"Slocum, I'll want to go with you. Take me with you, please?"

"Leave all this power and the place you've got here?"

"I'd go with you."

"And do what? Sure, you would sleep out under the stars, freeze in the winter and bake in the summer. Why, we could stop over at bedbug hotels and fleabag wagon yard bunks. When you got tired of beans, we could gnaw on jackrabbits so tough that boot-sole leather would be like a spring chicken in comparison."

"I have money."

"Yes, and when it's gone, and money always expires like the sun goes down, then we can work some two-bit outfit for a banker and break horses for spending money. No, you can't make those kind of plans with me."

"I want to be with you." She snuggled as close to him as she could to absorb the heat from his body. Her shaking had subsided some, and the sun was focused on the nook in the hills that they shared with the falls. Slocum closed his eyes for a second, then, with a finger, sorted strands of her hair as he looked down at the top of her head. Helluva mess. He drew a deep breath up his nostrils for strength.

He parted with her before the moon began to rise. Spent and uncertain of his true enemy, he pushed Dunny northward toward Champion's place. He planned to catch some sleep at Nat's, then head for Buffalo and see how well his plans for the major were working out. His eyelids heavy as if they were lead-filled, he sagged in the saddle, only to bolt up right when he threatened to lose his seat as he pushed Dunny northward. He saw no lights on at Nat's cabin when he unsaddled. They all must have spent the night in Buffalo, too tired to go any further. He rolled out a bedroll in the shed and went to sleep in the hay.

He woke to the hurrahs and shouting of three or so riders. They had Nat's horses on the run from the pens before he could find his pistol. He rushed out in the starlight and began to shoot at the outlines of the rustlers. His bullets silenced their shouts, and they quickly reined away into the night as if they had not expected any opposition. He punched fresh rounds into his Colt, cursing that not one of his shots had stopped a rustler that he could see.

He found Dunny, who had come back to the barn. In haste, he saddled him and rode out in the moonlight to gather the horses he could find. They couldn't be far, because he had stopped the raiders before they got them much more than out of the corral. Come daylight, he would look and see what he could tell about their hoof-marks. Damn, who were these horse-chousers? They had even shaken the Indian tracker. There had to be something to their phantom ways. The tracker had found nothing to indicate their whereabouts. Slocum had thought all the time that they had circled back to Imagene's place. What if she wasn't lying to him? Hell, she had to be. He was letting his horniness direct his brain. Simple enough.

16

"Guess what?" Nicky asked as Slocum joined them at the wagon yard in Buffalo. He saw Nat and Etta, but there was no sign of Jen or the lawyer Crocker in the group fixing to mount up.

Slocum shook his head in reply to the youth. "I can't."

"They ain't having roundup until the major gets better." Nick grinned smugly.

"He sick?" Slocum asked as he dismounted.

"They think he may have chol-eeria."

"Reckon he'll live?" he asked for the benefit of the rest of the ranchers gathered around.

"I hope the old sum-bitch shits himself to death," one of the men said, and a chorus of "amens" followed.

"He came down with it last night, and they say he don't dare leave sight of the thunder mug in his hotel room," another man said.

"Yeah and he must be in misery," Nicky added.

"That man of his has been here already once today to get him some more whiskey. I sure hope it ain't contagious, whatever he's got."

"Well, I'm going home and round up the rest of my horses," one of the ranchers announced. "I'll be ready to ride by the time he gets over this disease."

"Wait," Slocum said to some preparing to depart. "They struck Nat's pens last night and tried to scatter his horses."

"Everyone of them FXT hands was in the Wild Horse Saloon," Shorty said, pushing his horse in to where Slocum stood. "I know. I checked on them twice last night, figuring they were the ones doing it. So who's behind it?"

"I'm not sure," Slocum said with a shake of his head. All of her men were in the saloon last night? No one could ride from Buffalo to Nat's in less than a few hours. And their horses would have been obviously winded. Damn, that stubborn Imagene wasn't lying to him.

"You look deep in thought, pard," Nat said, coming over with Etta on his arm.

"Lots of things don't add up," Slocum said, lowering his voice. "Shorty just said that the FXT boys were all here in town. Three riders tried to drive off your remuda last night."

"They made it look like they were all here, I'd bet," Nat scoffed.

"No, I think there's more to this than meets the eye. The answer may lie with the major, and he won't tell us nothing." He rubbed the beard stubble on his cheek with his index finger, and tried to think how he could trip up one of the major's men to get some answers. The problem was, they probably didn't know a thing. He needed to find where the horse-chasers were hiding out. Nat wouldn't be any great assistance, he was too struck on Etta. Slocum could write his friend off as any help.

"Well, the major ain't going to be no trouble for a while." Nat shook his head, amused enough almost to laugh out loud.

"I don't see what is so funny about the man's illness," Etta said. "Every time his name comes up, Nat goes to laughing."

"Oh, he's enjoying the man's discomfort," Slocum assured her. Where was Jenny? Maybe she knew a place where the raiders could be hiding?

"You get out on bond?" Slocum asked his friend.

"Sure did. That lawyer Crocker is getting on the stage," Nat said. "He's coming back for the trial in three weeks. He even got a court order that bars the major from blacklisting me from the roundup."

"Good, I need to check on a thing or two," Slocum said, and swung back up on Dunny. If Jenny was putting Crocker on the stage, perhaps he could talk to her when she finished. Full of dread over the notion of a meeting with her, for he knew she had no doubt by this time met Etta, he nodded good-bye to Nat, Etta, and the others.

"You coming out to the ranch?" Nat asked after him.

"Yes, after I do a few things. I'll see you there." He booted Dunny out the yard gate and up the street for the stage stop.

A block up the street, he saw the stagecoach parked beside a porch. He jogged the dun across the hollow plank bridge. The warmth of the morning sun was on his chest and right leg as he rode toward the vehicle. He halted Dunny short of the stage line's office when he saw Jen and a man who had to be Crocker talking on the porch. Taking his time to hitch the reins, he waited until the lawyer mounted the coach steps and went inside before he stepped on the boardwalk and headed for her.

"Slocum," she said, turning from waving at the departing Crocker.

"Morning, Jen."

"I wondered where you were at during all the fun." She forced a smile for him. "The major is very sick and the doctor can't figure out why. He says he has some kind of intestinal problem that even Black Draught can't cure. They have him on a diet of browned flour, according to my information."

"Must be bad," Slocum said, looking past her as he studied two familiar hipshot horses in front of Hennesey's. Both had been ridden hard, but the far one interested him the most. It was an Appalousa, and even in Wyoming they were scare. It was a horse that the Nez Percé in the Northwest had bred up. The spots on the black animal's white-patched rump were distinctive. He could only belong to one man—Lyle Abbot. And that meant the other horse with the dried lather on him belonged to Dirk Abbot. The Ft. Scott, Kansas, bounty hunters were in Buffalo and within a hundred fifty feet of him.

He drew Jen into the alley. His time was short.

"What's the matter?" she asked.

"I need to know where a half-dozen riders can hide and not an Indian can find them."

"Is something wrong?" she asked.

"I haven't time to explain much to you, but there are two men across the street in the saloon that I don't want to know I'm here."

"Who are they?" She frowned at him.

"I don't have time, Jen."

"Did you see that—woman he's with?" Her eyes opened wide, demanding his reply.

"Etta Watson, yes," he said grimly. "I tried to warn you."

"Damn, she's nothing but a—" His fingertips closed off her words.

"I don't have time to talk about Nat's love life here. You go out and lead Dunny around here in the alley.

Then we can go on the side street to Mrs. Hawkins' barn and talk. I need to get out of here for the moment.''

''Who are those men?'' She frowned at his caution.

''Bounty hunters, and I don't have time to kill them here.''

''I'll get Dunny,'' she said, her face paling under its tan.

He waited anxiously for her to come back so they could get moving. The Abbot brothers' appearance in the Powder River country put a new fly in the ointment for him. Something had told him he didn't need to show up with the posse protecting Nat. A good thing too. Still, there were plenty of folks in Buffalo who knew him by name when the Abbots went to asking around. He would have to watch his back trail a lot closer.

Before he left the basin, he was determined to find the horse-chasers and settle with them. If they weren't FXT hands, then he had eliminated one set of rannies. He hated that he had not believed Imagene. At least he knew she had been honest with him. Whatever that meant in a senseless relationship between two torrid people.

''Who are they?'' Jen asked in a whisper, leading Dunny by the bridle reins.

''Lyle and Dirk Abbot from Ft. Scott, Kansas.''

''What do they want you for?'' she asked as he looked over his shoulder. Nothing behind them. Those two were probably nursing a big thirst in the saloon.

''A long time ago I got into a scrap. Here, mount up, he'll carry double,'' he said, satisfied they were out of the view of the saloon. She grasped the horn and swung into the saddle; he came behind her, straightened himself with the cantle, and settled in.

''It was one of those bad deals. Certain folks owned the law and a Texas puncher had no rights, so I hiked out of there. Those same folks must have a pocket full of money to keep those two dogging me.''

"They ever catch you?"

"I'm here, aren't I?"

She shook her head, and put Dunny across the plank bridge. Slocum twisted and looked back to be certain they weren't being followed. Then he turned back, satisfied that he needed to depart Buffalo and begin his search for the raiders.

"You have any idea where they could be hiding?" he asked.

"Who?"

"We eliminated the FXT boys from the list. All of them were here last night when a bunch hit Nat's place while I was up there."

"Who are they, then?"

"Hired guns, I'd say." He dismounted behind Mrs. Hawkins's small barn.

"Who hired them?"

"I'd guess the Cheyenne Social Club and the major."

"You sure that Imagene Furston's not behind it?" she asked, jumping down. Then she patted the dun on the neck. "Heckuva good horse."

"I'm not sure of anything. Yes, he's the best pony I've owned in a spell. Think where they could be hiding out."

"There's a medicine wheel up on the Bighorns, and beyond that is some real rough country I guess only the Indians know about. You can sure get lost up there, but I've heard there's a place back there called Hole-in-the-Wall that's a hideout."

"They could be up there?"

"It's one of those places that people don't come back from." She shrugged and looked down at her boot toes as if considering the matter. "Yes, that could be their hideout. Where are you going?"

"To find the Hole-in-the-Wall," he said, swinging up on his horse.

"Wait, I want to go too." She looked at him hard enough. "Don't tell me it ain't a place for a girl. We can get a packhorse at our place and I'll get enough supplies for two weeks."

"You'll need to be back for roundup before then," he reminded her.

"You're right," she said in defeat. "I still can go get you those supplies and then meet you at my place. You'll need them."

"Here, take this money." He leaned down with the money to give it to her.

"Go on. I'll meet you at the ranch." She waved away his offer as she went inside for her own horse.

"See you," he said, and trotted Dunny for the valley. Things in his life had a way of turning crossways about the time he needed obstacles less than anything. A picture of the Abbot brothers only made him madder; he needed them around like a case of the piles. A big pain in the butt was all they were, but they could be the death of him too. He booted Dunny into a short lope for the Van Doren place.

"So, the major has the loose bowels?" Emil asked, amused, as Slocum reset the front shoes on Dunny. He wanted him sound to go into the mountains where a slip could cost both of them their lives.

"They tell me it is a serious disease and he's not getting over it," Slocum said.

"A couple of boys rode by and told me he was too puny to even sit a horse."

"Black Draught never even cut it," Slocum said, driving new nails in the left hoof cupped in his lap.

"Couldn't happen to a finer fellow. Where are you going?"

"I think the horse raiders are hiding over the Big-horns. Jenny mentioned the medicine wheel and some-place called Hole-in-the-Wall."

"Damn tough country. I've heard some of Sitting Bull's renegade bucks stay back there."

"Well, we eliminated the FXT bunch as the main troublemakers. They were all in town last night when someone raided Nat's place. I ran them off before they did much damage."

"Damn, who are they?" Emil asked, resting on his crutches.

"Hired guns, I figure." He dropped the hoof and straightened his stiff muscles. He still had another plate to reset. He looked up as Jen rode into view pushing her bay hard.

"Something on fire?" Emil asked her when she drew up before them. Two large white cloth sacks bulging with goods hung over her legs.

"No, but I wanted to get back before he rode off without any supplies. They're going to start roundup Thursday," she said, out of breath. "Sending someone named Dukes to take the major's place."

"Most folks will be ready," Slocum said, bent over with the right hoof in his hand and prying the shoe free with the short-handled hammer's claws.

"Those two men were still in the saloon when I left."

"Good," he said, without looking up from his chore as the nails began to give. Soon the shoe came free, and he dropped the horse's foot and rose up, looking at the flatness of the shoe.

"I don't think you should go into those mountains by yourself," she said with dread in her voice.

"I've been taking care of myself for a long time." He used a pair of pinchers to remove the bent nails, then battered the plate flat with his hammer on the anvil until satisfied with his corrections.

"You can stay the night, can't you?" she asked.

He checked the sun time. Not much time left in the day anyway, and he still had to redo this hoof. It didn't matter when he left. A good night's rest and then he could hit the owlhoot's trail over the crest, if there was one.

"Persistent, isn't she?" Emil handed him the rasp and smiled as she headed for the house.

"She may not tell you, but Nat found this Etta Watson in Story and she's moved in on him." Slocum used the rasp to shape the foot. As he made long swipes, the teeth took shreds of excess hoof material with each pass until the surface satisfied him.

"Maybe she'll come to her senses about him," Emil said.

"I doubt it. But she's taking it better than I expected."

"Heavens, he doesn't even know that she exists."

"Still, I think she's hiding a big part of her feelings." He set down the horse's foot to get some relief from the pain in his lower back. Hands on his hips, he went to the bench for some nails. Shoeing never use to be this tough. Then he remembered his recent tryst with the subtle Imagene, and nodded to himself. It wasn't horseshoeing that was killing him.

Supper proved a congenial feast. Jen had fried some young chickens in a brown crust that made the last piece as mouthwatering as the first. No burned biscuits. They were light and fluffy as clouds, and the flour gravy was thick and perfect on her potatoes. He was unable to eat another bite, but then she delivered an apple crisp from the oven that nearly floated his tongue away. After two dishes of it, he sat back, too full to burp, ready to help her with dishes when she shoed him off with Emil to the fireplace chairs.

"Where's Nat's girl come from?" Emil asked, soft enough that she couldn't hear them as she was busy rattling dishes in the wash pan.

"Chelsey's."

"Oh." Emil dismissed it with a wave of his hands. That matter settled, they talked about cattle prices and the benefits of new bloodlines.

She joined them, and spoke of the lawyer Crocker and his plans to call in every basin rancher to testify in favor of Nat until the judge made them stop. Obviously the man had made an impression on her, for she sounded very hopeful when she brought up each point about the lawyer.

"He's going to fight them in Congress too," she said.

"They want new laws to outlaw us?" Emil asked.

"They won't ever give up," she said, and rose to put a log on the small fire driving out the evening chill in the big room. "I think that folks have a real fighter in this Crocker."

"Sounds that way. I'm going to get some sleep. Good to have you home to cook, girl. Slocum, you watch yourself up there. Lots of men ain't come back from there." He maneuvered the crutches under his armpits, then shook hands with him.

"Thanks for everything," Slocum said, watching the man hobble off to the side room door.

"I sure wish you could stay around." Emil said, stopping and swinging around. "I think you got the best of the major, and that's never been done before. Good job." He left on his crutches and closed the door behind himself.

"Those two bounty hunters, there isn't a thing that can be done about them?" Jen asked, looking at her hands in her lap.

"No. I'll see if I can't run these raiders off for all of you. Then I need to ride on."

"No wife? No kids?" She looked deep in his eyes, then went to rocking.

"No hearth of my own to sit by on a chilly night either." He looked over at her as she went back and forth in the straight-backed rocker.

"You must miss having something, some place where you can sit and not worry about the likes of them slipping up on you."

"I do, but there hasn't been a time for a lot of years when I don't have to ride on."

"It won't ever get better?" she asked.

He shook his head, and then stared at the huge moose rack over the fireplace.

"There are things, Jen, that can't ever be made right again. And some folks have a notion how they think it happened, and that won't ever change no matter how wrong they are."

"I want a favor from you." She stopped rocking and observed the closed door to his bedroom.

"What's that?"

"Come with me," she said, and took him by the hand. At the front door, she put on a shawl, and he slipped on his jumper.

Then she led him outside, and across the star lit yard, speaking to the curious cow dogs that came to accompany them.

"This is the bunkhouse," she said, opening the door.

He struck a match, and she set up the candle on the table for him to light. Then she kneeled at the small stove and tossed in kindling and shavings. He joined her, and ignited the wood with another match. On their haunches, they waited in silence for the flames to lick up and blaze. One at a time, she added sticks of split wood until satisfied that her fire was going.

The two of them straightened and she hugged him,

burying her face in his chest. He held her loose in his arms and waited for her to speak.

"I want you to make me a woman," she said.

"You are one, Jenny."

"No, Slocum, don't put me off."

"Why me?"

"Because I've decided that you must surely know how to treat a woman. You understand my feelings about Nat. I know I can't have him, but he'll be around here to remind me what a fool I was over him. I want a memory of you."

"Why not wait for the right man?"

"Am I ugly? Repulsive?"

"No."

"Then I am yours. How do you start?"

"Like this," he said, convinced that she would chicken out on him before he went far.

His mouth sought hers, and her stiff lips barely moved as he held her tight to his body and savored her willowy form in his arms. Then her mouth parted, and soon he was tasting the honey in it. Her breathing increased, and her arms wrapped around his neck.

The dogs began to bark. He paused and listened as she panted for breath.

"Someone's coming in," he said, standing her on her feet. In an instant, he blew out the candle and, Colt in hand with her on his heels, opened the bunkhouse door. The dogs were really barking at the shadowy riders by the corral.

"Horse raiders, stay here!" he said to her, seeing them in the starlight by the corrals. The dogs were raising a ruckus at the intruders.

A shot flashed red, and one of the cow dogs yelped in pain.

"Damn them!" she swore as he caught her with his outflung arm to stop her.

"Reach for the sky!" he shouted, shoving her behind a wagon box with his gun hand and expecting to draw their fire.

Suddenly the night was full of cursing and wild shots striking all around, and he fired twice and then dove behind a pile of lumber. He stood up as the raiders jerked their panicked horses around and began to flee. A shotgun blast from the porch sent two of their mounts bucking out of the yard.

Slocum was on his feet firing his last three shots after the fleeing raiders.

"You all right, Emil?" Jen shouted, running for the house.

"Hell, it'll take more than a shotgun recoil to hurt me," the man said with a laugh.

The sound of his voice made Slocum feel better as he closed the gate. The horses were still inside. Between the dogs and them, they had foiled another raid. And he had tracks to follow. The still form of the white and brown collie hurt him as he went by it.

He punched out the empties as he hurried to the house, reloading the chambers on his way. Emil was seated on a chair on the porch when he joined the two of them.

"Old ten-gauge knocked me off my pegs is all," Emil said. "One minute I was pulling the trigger, the next I was on my butt."

"You sure put some buckshot in their ponies' tails."

"Good. It was all worth it then."

"You sure that you're all right?" she asked.

"Here, we'll get you inside," Slocum said. "They won't be back for more tonight."

"I guess they got Tobie?" the man asked with a shake of his head.

"Yes, I'll bury him," Slocum offered as Emil got on his crutches and started inside with her helping him.

"Take a lamp," she said.

"Plenty of moonlight now," Slocum said, and let them go in the front door. Then he went after the shovel.

He had the hole deep enough to plant the stock dog when she came out with a blanket wrapped around her against the growing night wind.

"Your father all right?"

"Oh, he'll be stiff for a few weeks from the fall, but he's tough."

"Sorry about the dog," he said, lowering its body in the hole.

"He was a good one. Doing his job of defending the place too,"

"Gave his life for the outfit." He shoveled the dirt and gravel in on top of the corpse. He worked up a sweat to finish it, then drew a deep breath and leaned on the handle. A half-moon had risen in the east and cast its light on the junipers beside them and on her dark blanket.

"I bet the bunkhouse is warm by now," she said softly.

"You'd probably win that bet," he said, shouldering the shovel. Then he placed an arm on her shoulders as they started back. "You still want to find out?" he asked her.

"Yes."

17

Slocum closed his eyes, lost in the whirlpool of their passions. The velvet feel of Jen's smooth skin against his sent waves of electricity through his scrambled thoughts in the bunkhouse's darkness. Their shuddering breath rasped in the quiet room. With her underneath him on the narrow bunk, he was on fire with desire for her body. Her legs parted, and he eased himself into her. The soft cry from her parted lips was cut short as she tried in a frenzy to pull him down on top of her. He thrust himself deeper and deeper, their enthusiasm growing faster and wilder for more.

The narrow bunk creaked and complained as, higher and higher, they climbed the steepest angles, soaring like eagles. Never enough, never satisfied, wanting more and more, until they reached a ferocious whirling storm. Finally they slammed pelvis-to-pelvis in a final teeth-clenching effort of strain, and then, spent, they both fell in each other's arms, trembling, weak, and out of breath.

"Slocum? Am I still in one piece?"

"I don't know."

"I think I have been broken in two."

He raised up and playfully cupped one of her hard breasts. Bending over, he tenderly kissed the hard brown nipple and then smiled in the darkness at her. They managed to scoot around on the narrow bed until they lay side by side.

"I won't forget you."

"You better. I probably won't be back."

"I know you're the one that mothers warn their daughters about."

"I warned you too,"

"Thank God I never believed you," she said, and flung an arm over him and pressed herself to him. "Can we rest a while and do it again?"

"I guess." He shrugged as he gazed at the dark underside of the bunk above him. Maybe he could. Oh, hell, he had unleashed a fiery one.

"Good, I want all you have before you leave."

Dawn was a rosy orange on the far horizon. The packhorse loaded and Dunny saddled, he joined her in the main room.

"Emil wanted to sleep in. Says he's fine, just sore from his fall."

"You sure?" he asked, looking toward the closed bedroom.

"Take my word, he's a tough old bird."

"Good. You going to roundup tomorrow?"

"Yes. Nicky is coming by to help me get my horses in with Nat's and some of the others."

"Don't treat Etta too bad," he said, and reached over and squeezed her forearm. "She's determined to become a rancher."

"Determined to take Nat Champion for sure."

He frowned in disapproval at her words, and she relented with a shrug. Satisfied that he had defused her some, he started in on his fried eggs and the pile of flapjacks on his plate.

"I can't have him, she can. Besides . . ." She stopped and looked whimsically at Slocum. "Do you think I could ever make a certain Cheyenne lawyer look at me?"

"Why not?"

"What do I need to do?" She leaned across the table for his answer.

"Be yourself."

"Huh?" She narrowed her eyes in a look of distrust at him.

"Just because Nat couldn't see you is no sign that lawyer won't."

"You really think so?"

"Yes, I do. I saw you and him talking on the porch. That's the reason I didn't rush up there. I saw some sparks between the two of you."

"Sparks, huh? Slocum, you take care of yourself. You need help any time, I'm ready to do whatever you need. The folks up here owe you a lot."

"I need to vamoose. You rope that lawyer. I may need one some day. Good food. I've enjoyed myself."

"So did I," she whispered.

Jen put on her shawl, then took his arm and accompanied him to the horses. In the cool morning air, he kissed her good-bye, and then mounted his horse and took up the lead on the bay horse she had lent him.

He left her waving, and stood in the stirrups as he trotted Dunny on the tracks of the raiders. Somewhere up there in the snowy peaks towering above him, or on the other side of the Bighorns, they were in hiding and he intended to find them.

*   *   *

Noon found him letting the horses rest and graze in an alpine meadow. His appearance had sent a small herd of cow elks and their calves crashing off into the thick timber. He lounged on a blanket and watched a golden eagle soar by in his eternal search for food or carrion. Still weary from the lack of sleep and their night of passion, he closed his eyes as the horses chomped grass close by.

He awoke with a start. Hand on his gun butt, he forced himself up, searching around. Then he saw the source of the grunts. A sow black bear and two whining cubs were seeking grubs from a half-rotten stump. Her offspring ignored the fat white insects she uncovered with her long claws; they wanted milk. Each time they tried for a teat, she clubbed them aside end over end. Undeterred by the treatment, they came right back and tried again to suckle her. It became obvious that it was no use to hold them off any longer, so finally, when she realized the swipes were not going to deny the persistent pair, she gave up. With a loud grunt, she lay down on her side and the two attacked her. Their nosy sucking carried to Slocum across the clearing.

Later, he re-did the cinches on both horses and then stepped into the saddle. On his way again, he had raiders' tracks in mind as he rode upward toward the peaks; the air grew colder by the mile.

In late evening, he crossed a divide, bare save for the short grass that the wind swept and waved. There on the ground he discovered the wagon wheel of rocks laid out by some ancient people. Boulders formed the outer circle, and smaller ones made up the spokes. He dismounted and stretched his legs as he examined the works of earlier men. Probably done by people who had never seen a wagon wheel. It was a sign to their deity, something he could not understand.

A place to pray to their god. Small presents still dotted the area, especially the outer boulders. He remounted

Dunny as a cold shiver went up his spine. How could he use this wheel? It meant nothing to him, but perhaps the medicine—he could use the strength it must give to the observer. If only he knew how to unlock the secret.

In his lifetime, he had lived with various witches. They were of different origins and religions; Mexican, Apache, Shoshone, Comanche, and Sioux. There was no reason for him to ever deny any of their beliefs. They were all stronger than he was in metaphysical ways.

"Ring of life," he asked, removing his hat as the wind drowned his voice like some great spirit, stronger and more powerful than a mere man. The force held him in its palm. "Be with me?"

Then the wind died down as if set aside by some great hands, and the short grass around the circle of rocks stood still. In respect, he bowed his head and shut his eyelids. If this was his blessing, then he accepted it, and finally he raised his gaze to the purple vastness beyond. His hat in place, he booted Dunny on, leading the pack-horse behind. The moment passed, but in his gut he felt something that he was unsure about—he had been touched by the spirit of the Bighorn's medicine wheel and he would never be the same again.

Close to sundown on the far slope, he made a camp for himself in a grove of stunted lodgepoles a good ways from the trail. He'd learned lots about whom he tracked, the men and the mounts they rode. Twice, he had lost their trail, but after the medicine wheel experience he seemed to be able almost to point out their direction of travel. It led southwest, and he wondered if they were leaving the country. They were far enough away that a raid back in the basin would not be a simple overnight trip.

One of them rode a pigeon-toed horse; his boots needed re-heeling and the nails showed in his tracks. A second one wore moccasins, the third man flat heels.

One had two new plates on the front of his mount. That was the flat-heeled rider. They didn't overly try to hide their tracks, and seemed to be using a fairly well-defined trail.

He made a small fire, cooked dry beans and coffee, and tried to imagine what he would find ahead. They obviously had a place, a hideout, to stay in. How did they know when to come out and do things? There were lots of unanswered questions in this business.

He sat back and listened as a wolf's deep throaty howl cut the cool night air. Then another answered. Big wolves with an appetite to fill. Then other pack members joined in. They must have cut the trail of mule deer or other game and charged down the mountainside. With plenty for them to eat up here, they would avoid his small fire unless driven by hunger. But this pack would pull down a deer or mountain sheep before the night was over. Then they would ravage the carcass, snarling at each other to enforce their strict social code of higher and lower castes.

He listened to the pack's cries until they went from his hearing. An owl floated by, hooting and searching for a nocturnal meal. Slocum undid his bedroll and crawled inside. Somewhere ahead, the raiders were camped. He would be glad when he found them and could ride on.

18

He stood in the stirrups, trotting down the slope. The prints here were obviously fresh. Then a powerful slap struck the dun horse in the chest. He stopped, stumbled, then went down to his knees. The report of the rifle carried on the thin air as Slocum shucked his stirrups and instinctively dove for the ground. He had found the raiders, or worse, they had discovered him. On top of that they had taken out Dunny, who struggled and grunted in death throes on his side. Slocum crawfished on his belly to get behind the security of Dunny's bulk. As he tried to ascertain the direction of the shooter, he cursed his luck. He had twisted his ankle in the jump and he knew it would be sore, but far worse than that, he realized that his rifle was pinned under the dying dun. There was no way to get it free without exposing himself.

As if Dunny's death wasn't enough, the bay pack-horse took the opportunity to flee all the bullets that ricocheted around them. From his place on the ground, Slocum watched it hightail around a grove of scrub pines and then race up his back trail. A fine fix he had gotten himself in. Colt in his hand, he waited behind the dead horse as the high mountain winds made shrill whistles in his ear.

An occasional shot intended for him struck the horse's corpse, or went screaming off over his head across the mountain after chipping a rock or making a puff of dust close by. They had him pinned down, and all they had to do was wait. Grimacing in pain, he flexed the sore ankle, already swelling inside his boot. He had no supplies, his long gun was underneath the horse, and he was afoot. All things so far added up to an ending that he didn't like to contemplate. There was an answer to every problem, but he wasn't that certain how this one would end.

If he could make it until dark, then there might be a chance to escape on his sore ankle. On foot, he could lose the ordinary person, but whether the leg would support him was another thing. The Indian in their outfit might make a difference. Slocum decided the moccasin wearer was either a breed or full blood. That could be a harder one to lose. So far, he knew little more than the fact there were three of them out there. If they dared get careless, then he could manage to eliminate one or more of them. He slapped the gun barrel in his palm— chances of that were slim to none.

He planned to wait before he looked over the horse's form until they had time to tire of aiming their rifles in his direction. They probably were simply waiting for his appearance to pull the trigger. What else could he do? Nothing came to his mind. The rocks under his back were as uncomfortable as his sore foot was becoming.

An eagle screamed. He saw its shadow pass over, but the bird itself was too far south for him to see without exposing himself. The sun's warmth felt good as he soaked it up. He rolled over to let his back soak up some of the solar power. This would be his world, belly-down or lying on his back and keeping his head down.

A shot slapped nearby, and he resumed his thinking. Even if he could run, his pistol would be no match for their long-range weapons. From here on he had to be certain that they didn't sneak around him. That was what *he* would do, circle to get in position for a clear shot.

He listened for any sounds. Damn, this would be a long day without food or drink. Then he heard the horse scrambling. One of them was going to circle around as he suspected. The rider was urging his mount on.

Slocum took a position on his stomach. Pistol cocked, he knew he had one chance to stop the ambusher. His eyes narrowed as the horse to the west struggled on the hillside. Then the mount's brown head appeared, and the dark face of the breed on his back showed in a space between the boughs. It was enough of a view. He emptied his pistol and the rider spilled off backwards, his handgun shooting harmlessly into the sky.

No time to watch for what happened next, Slocum punched out the casings and reloaded as fast as he could. When he looked up again, he could see the bay pony, head down as he grazed, trailing his reins. There was no sign of his rider. Only the wind in the pine needles carried to Slocum.

"Breed?" someone shouted. "You all right?"

No answer.

A wounded breed was a worse threat than a rattler. Slocum only hoped he had ended the man's life, not simply wounded him. The situation had become life or death, and he wasn't satisfied with their plans to make him the victim. A few more bullets skipped around him. So far the horse's bulk had kept him safe.

Day dragged into night. They made no more moves.

The breed obviously had gone on to his ancestors. Slocum could hear the other two talking, but couldn't make out what they said. Whiffs of their wood smoke made his empty stomach complain.

"Give yourself up!" someone ordered.

"Come get me!" Slocum shouted back.

"We will, you son of a bitch!"

That terminated their conversation, and the sun set.

19

The night's chill caused his teeth to chatter. He had tried to use his leg, but it was too swollen to carry him far. Twice he had slipped around beside the horse to try to get his rifle out of the scabbard, but all he could reach was the end of the stock. The entire weight of the animal was on the Winchester. His actions drew some wild shots from the shooters, so he was forced to scoot back behind his fortress. They had him pinned down, and he couldn't figure out how he would ever get away, except in a pine box, and they weren't liable to worry about burying him.

Of all the close calls he'd had in his life, this looked like the toughest. Two hired guns, and they were taking turns standing guard. He had no one to spell him, and no blankets either.

Knife in hand, he raised up, leaving no silhouette, and sliced the bedroll strings. Keeping low so he did not make a target, he tugged with all his might at the roll, but the weight of the horse held it solid.

He might freeze without it. He strained harder, hoping the ties underneath would give. Two bullets slapped into the horse in sickening fashion. He dropped behind again and caught his breath, grateful they couldn't see him well enough in the starlight to shoot him.

His breathing normal again, he eased himself up and reached over to pull on the roll. He thought it came some. If he could raise up high enough, use both hands, maybe he could wrestle the blankets free. On his knees, he dared to pull with both arms grasping the blankets, and with a great effort they came loose. He sprawled on his back with his prize on his chest in his hug. At least he might not freeze.

"He's trying something up there!" One of the shooters said.

"Come daylight, we'll flush him," the other voice said.

"Get ready to die," Slocum said to himself as he spread the blankets over himself. "I'm taking one or both of you with me."

He would be glad when his body heat collected enough under the covers to stop his shaking. If it didn't happen soon, he might break his teeth, he was chattering them so hard. A mess, a real mess.

He wondered as heat finally returned if he could crawl out to the breed and get his gun. It would be slow, there wouldn't be as much cover out there, but under a dark blanket, he might be able to get there.

Crab-like he began to ease himself on his knees to the grove of trees where the breed had fallen. Every rustle, every scuffle that he made sounded like thunder. Finally in the shadows of the pines, still undiscovered, he looked around for the breed's horse. He squinted his eyes and listened. There was no sign of the animal as he sat with his back to a small pine trunk.

Where was the damn breed's body? They had not even come to see about it. Typical backshooters. They'd sent the breed up to kill him and when he'd failed, they'd written him off. Then twenty feet away, he saw a sprawled form between some sagebrush.

One thing he could use was the breed's gun. Satisfied that he was out of the view of the other two, he half limped and dragged the sore leg until he was beside the body. The handgun glistened in the starlight. He bent over and swept the Colt up, jammed it in his waistband, and went to strip the breed of his gunbelt. That gave him twice the gun power, though a rifle would be better. But there was no sign of the horse or anything, except the stiff body of the dead man.

It left him with perhaps thirty more cartridges and one more weapon. Anything for an advantage over his adversaries. He looked around. There was no place out there to hide. He was disappointed with his bad ankle, which left him no choice but to accept the fact that he could not outrun them. Carefully he moved back to the dead horse and then, once secure again in his fortress, he reloaded the second Colt with six shells. Then he wrapped himself in his blankets. Both revolvers close at hand, he waited for dawn.

He was half awake and trying to listen when the pre-dawn on the mountaintop was shattered with the cannon report of a ten-gauge. It delivered a second round over his head as he frowned, puzzled. But the flying pine needles shattered over his adversaries' heads drew a scream out of them, and he heard them rush for their mounts.

Reloaded, the ten-gauge cut down on them again as Slocum hugged the ground, to keep out of the path of the fistful of buckshot whistling over his head. The shooters were whipping their horses to flee off the mountaintop.

"That you, Emil?" he asked, lying on his stomach.

"That you, Slocum?"

"Yes, sir."

"You shot up?"

"No, but I have a bad swollen ankle."

"I'm coming as soon as I remount old Curly. He was the only horse I could use for a tripod for this blunderbuss."

In a few minutes, Emil came in view on a bay horse. The long-Tom shotgun was across his lap, and the gray-mouthed horse showed his age but he looked sound enough. Slocum had pulled himself up to sit on Dunny's corpse.

"Who were they?" Emil asked.

"Two of the three roughs that shot Dunny here and had me pinned down. One's dead over there." Slocum jerked his head toward the dead breed.

"When that packhorse came back, I saddled up Curly and we came all night to get here. Think I got lost a couple of times, but I seen their smoke and the dun horse down, so I figured they had got you. So I cut loose a few rounds."

"You did great. Can Curly pull my saddle off Dunny here if I undo the stirrups? I hate to loose my saddle or leave it up here."

"Tie on and we'll give it a tug." Emil tossed him his lariat.

With effort he moved around and undid the girths, then threaded the loop in under the fork and noosed the horn. Then he limped around to give the tail of the rope to Emil.

"Can't tell whose the worst off, you or me." Emil grinned and wrapped the rope around the horn. He spurred the horse to back up, and Curly strained. The rig finally came out.

In hops, Slocum went to undo it. The rope undone, he tossed the end at Emil to recoil. In disgust, he shook his head as he studied the Winchester, the long gun he had craved for twelve hours. The stock was shattered at the back of the receiver. One more thing that pair owed him for besides Dunny.

"What do you want to do?" Emil asked.

"Go back and start over," Slocum said.

"I'll go get the other horse I brought to bring your body in on."

"Glad I'm still alive," he shouted after him.

Emil reined up and twisted around. "I'm glad too. I don't know if I could have loaded you dead on a horse."

Slocum rolled up his bedroll and prepared for the man's return. His sore ankle would mend, but he owed those two for a lot of things. He didn't want to think about the loss of his horse Dunny. That alone was un-called for. He was thinking of forms of torture suitable for the two raiders when Emil came back leading an-other cow pony.

"He's past twenty, but Socks is easy to catch," Emil said.

"He'll do fine," Slocum said, setting his pads and then the rig on the almost swaybacked gelding. He reached under and cinched him up, slapped on the blan-kets, and tied them on one side that had strings. He jammed the busted rifle in the scabbard and swung aboard.

Socks may have been twenty, but his claim to fame was he hadn't been ridden by anyone in five years, and he broke in half. In the saddle, Slocum, half awake, re-alized that the swaybacked old cow pony intended to throw him at the moon. He sawed at his jaws, but the iron mouth was plunging out through the pines, which whipped at him as he tried his best to haul up the wildest old pony he could remember.

Then he lost a stirrup and the antics of the horse grew harder. A pine bough stout enough not to bend caught Slocum and swept him off the horse's back. Then it unceremoniously broke and deposited him on the ground.

Emil raced after the loose culprit, and came back leading the docile Socks. Slocum, meanwhile, had managed to get to his feet using the pine bough for support.

"I think he's over his spell."

"Good," Slocum said, not knowing whether to laugh or cry. He caught the check strap on Sock's bridle as he mounted, and the old cow pony could only circle, which he soon tired of, and then they were ready to ride.

"I got some jerky," Emil said as they rode side by side.

"I'd take some," Slocum said. He couldn't remember when he'd eaten anything last.

"You know," Emil said, handing the wrap of oilskin over to him.

"What's that?"

"I'd like to have a picture of old Socks when he sunfished with you."

"What would you have done with it?" Slocum asked.

"I'd sell him to one of them Wild West show guys as a big bucker."

Slocum began to laugh. Then Emil laughed too, until both men were doubled over.

"Sell old Socks for a bucker, huh?" Slocum said. The jerky he chewed drew the saliva in his mouth. Things had to go better. He wondered as they skirted the medicine wheel if he had been cursed instead of blessed by the ancient ones' shrine. What else would go wrong?

20

The dogs had been barking and woke him. He listened to the night wind on the corners of the bunkhouse. His third night back, his ankle was still swollen, and he'd been forced to use an extra pair of Emil's crutches. He raised his head to listen closer. The dogs had stopped raising Cain, so it probably was only some coyotes slinking around trying to catch a chicken. The two stock dogs were good sentinels, and it was a shame the raiders had shot the third. Slocum rolled over and nestled his head in the pillow with his back to the starlight spilling in the small windows.

"Make one move and you're dead," the raspy voice of Lyle Abbott ordered as he burst in the door.

At the sight of Lyle's bulk filling the doorway, slowly Slocum closed his eyes and wondered how they'd gotten by the dogs. He knew by the sounds of the other boots on the floor that there were more than the two brothers crowding into the room.

Someone struck a match in his face, and then he recognized the next voice.

"Hell, it's him. Pay us," Ferral said.

"Yes, we found him for you," Dave said. "We knowed he was up here after we followed that bitch up here last Sunday and seen he was here."

"I'll have to wire the sheriff in Ft. Scott and have him send you your part."

"You said cash on delivery," Ferral said, getting his back up.

"Hell, boys," Slocum said, swinging his sore ankle over the side of the bunk. "Them jayhawkers won't pay you nothing."

"What's he saying?" Dave demanded.

"Shut up, Slocum," Lyle threatened.

"This is a private war between me and them. They ain't with the law no way—" The lights went out when Lyle struck him with his pistol barrel on the top of the head, and he barely recalled falling face-down on the floor.

He came to, but stayed still as Lyle counted out money on the table for Ferral and Dave. Good, that had cost him a headache, but it had almost had them fighting among themselves. He chose to lay still and play out of it since he couldn't figure a way to agitate the rannies against the two brothers. He would have to start his brain working on how he was going to get away from them.

Lyle locked Slocum's hands behind his back, and the cuffs pinched when he snapped them as tight as he could in the last notch.

"We've got him," Lyle said, as excited as a little kid opening his Christmas present.

"Damn right, we've been after your ass for a long time, Slocum, you know that," Dirk said as he danced around the room. Finally he stopped and leaned over Slocum's prostrate form on the floor.

"A Pinkerton man saw you in Cheyenne a couple of weeks ago and wired us. It was only a matter of time until we got your ass." Dirk punctuated the sentence with a savage boot toe to Slocum's ribs. "Figure your way out of this one."

"I guess we better drag him out and on that horse we brung," Lyle said. "The sooner that he's in the Buffalo jail, the sooner we can get drunk and celebrate."

"That's right. We're rich after all these years!" Dirk said. His eyes gleamed in the candlelight.

"Shut up about that," Lyle warned him.

"No more cheap whores, bad whiskey! Slocum, I could dance all the way back to Buffalo. You've made us rich men."

"Well, damn, I'm proud you two chicken-shits can crawl out from under the roost and join the big turds in this world."

"Don't hit him again," Lyle warned his brother, who had his gun out. "He's heavy enough to load in the shape he's in."

"What happened to you anyway?" Dirk asked Slocum.

"Twisted my ankle looking for some killers and my horse was shot out from under me."

"Killers, ha! Only killer I see in this room is you." Dirk pointed. "And you're on your way to a big trial and a long-awaited Kansas hanging."

"Help me get him on the horse," Lyle said, impatient with all the talk.

"Damn, can't he help some?" Dirk grunted as they dragged him out of the bunkhouse and put him on the horse in the starlight. Ferral and Dave had taken their reward and left.

In the saddle, he looked to the dark house. Had Emil heard anything?

"He can't help you. That old man in the house is tied

up. He can get loose in a while. Tough old bastard, but he ain't hurt.''

"He better not be,'' Slocum said as they began to lead his horse. He strained at having his hands cuffed behind his back; they'd pay for any harm they did to Emil.

"Your threats ain't scaring me none. Your days as a free man are over, Slocum,'' Lyle said, and booted his Appalousa to make him hurry.

"Yeah, and we're going to be so damn rich that we can do anything we want to for the rest of our life,'' Dirk said.

"On a thousand dollars?'' Slocum scoffed. "I could pay you boys twice that much to set me free.''

"Where you got that kind of money?''

"Tombstone bank.''

"You never had two bits in your whole life.''

"You can wire them and ask if I have a safety deposit box in their vaults.'' He rode the horse, wincing at the pain in his foot as it hung down. He was unable to put it in the stiruup as the stiff-gaited horse tried to avoid Dirk's quirt and keep close to Lyle's Appalousa.

"Why in the hell you got money in one of them boxes?''

"Shut up, Dirk, he's lying to you. He ain't got a pot to piss in or the window to throw it out.''

"Still, we could use the money.''

"Boys, it's there in the First State Bank of Arizona vault, and there's more if you act like gentlemen going after it. Like undoing my hands.''

"We ain't uncuffing you for ten thousand bucks. Probably be counterfeit anyway.'' Lyle used his spurs hard on the App to make him go faster.

"You boys' loss, my gain.''

"You ain't getting out of this alive,'' Lyle said, turning in the saddle to glare at him in the starlight. "You won't need it down in Hell anyway.''

"Make that damn fancy horse of yours go faster," Dirk said, looking over his shoulder as if he feared someone was on their trail.

"So them two card cheats told you about the dogs and all that?"

"Yeah, they were stupid," Lyle said. "But they knew we had to capture them dogs or you'd be warned."

"They mention how many dogs the man had?"

"Yeah, they said they used to have three of them pot-lickers, but one got shot."

"I quess they knew who shot it?"

"Shut up, Dirk! He's pumping answers out of you faster than a lizard crossing the road."

"What do you mean, Lyle?"

"Just shut up and ride. We can talk later."

"I just told him them those two knew all about that other dog getting shot and how to handle the rest of them."

"Wonder how they knew about the dog getting shot," Slocum said.

"None of your damn nosy business!" Lyle raged. "Dirk, whip his gawdamn horse."

"Whip your own damn horse, he's the one lagging back."

21

The jailhouse in Buffalo was in the courthouse base-
ment. Behind bars in his cell, Slocum sat on the iron
bunk and considered his next move. The Abbot brothers
had almost swallowed his Tombstone bank hoax before
they delivered him to the Johnson County jail for holding. Somehow they were getting paid a lot more than
the thousand-dollar reward for his return. How else were
they going to live an easy life of whoring and drinking
from then on? Someone had promised them big bucks
for his capture, and it must include getting him back
alive. Bounty hunters didn't mess with bringing in more
than decapitated heads for identity.

He studied the names on the walls of the cell. Joe
Raft, Shorty Bill, Arkansas Hank, Reb Smith, Billie Ca-
lahan. *Hung March 16th* followed the last name. There
were many obscene messages as well, like what needed
to be done to the sheriff.

"They won't set bond," Imagene said, looking at him grim-faced through the bars.

"I didn't expect they would," he said, easing his sore foot down and rising with some effort from the iron bed. Imagene Furston stood in a black riding outfit outside the cell.

"This isn't hardly the place for a lady," he said softly, glancing over at the two snoring drunks in the next cell.

"I'm a damn sight from being that."

"I wouldn't say that," he said, grasping the bars and looking down at her.

"You can say what you want. What can I do?"

"Forget about me."

"That's . . ." She looked back at the cell-block door and then at the other empty cells, avoiding his gaze. "Harder than I want to admit."

"You have a ranch. There's a million good men in this world."

"Shut up, I'm thinking. It's a miracle that your friends didn't bust down the door already."

"Gene, leave me and I'll manage somehow."

"Dammit, I don't give up on what I want."

"This time you lose. Thanks for coming." He started back for the cot. His ankle was becoming stronger. If the Abbot brothers stayed drunk a few more days, he would be able to use it to walk on.

"Slocum, I'm not giving up on getting you freed."

He shook his head to discourage her, and didn't turn to see her leave. Then there were the sounds of the soles of her hand-made boots on the stone-block floor as she left the cell block. He dropped his butt on the cot and shook his head. She was a hard female to shake.

*   *   *

"Put your hands out," Lyle ordered. "We're getting the hell out of here before your friends try to break you out."

He snapped the hancuffs on Slocum's wrist. It must be near midnight or past, he decided. The Abbots weren't taking any chances that Nat or Jen would do something to get him freed. They were taking him out in the middle of the night.

"My hat?" he asked, and nodded toward it. Lyle put the Stetson on his head, and Slocum managed to reset it more comfortably with his cuffed hands.

"Be glad to get him out of here," the old man on night duty at the jail said. "I think that you're smart to be getting him the hell out of Buffalo. Them small ranchers are sure pissed he's in here."

"Yeah, well, they can be pissed all they want," Lyle said, shoving Slocum toward the door. "We got horses outside to ride. Don't try anything smart, Slocum, or you're dead. You hear me?"

"I've got ears."

"Just so you don't get any idea that you can get away from us."

Slocum did not bother to answer him. His mind was on the long ride ahead back to Kansas. Somewhere he had to find a way to escape them. They would make a mistake—let their guard down. He recalled the long night behind the dead horse in the Bighorns, trying to stay awake, knowing that to leave the safety of Dunny's corpse on his weak ankle was more risk than he needed to take. The ankle was healed enough now to support him, so he was mobile. He needed a good plan.

"Mount up," Lyle ordered when they reached the horses.

Dirk sat on his mount with a rifle cradled in his arm as the lookout. They had a packhorse loaded to take along, Slocum noted as he swung up. The stirrups were short, but he didn't care. He clung to the horn as Lyle mounted and jerked Slocum's horse on a lead after his App. They left Buffalo on a high trot under the stars.

They'd ridden several miles when they entered a narrow place in the road. A gunshot broke the night's stillness. Out of nowhere, several white-hooded riders surrounded them.

"Hands in the air!" a loud voice shouted.

Slocum didn't recognize the voice. He raised his handcuffed hands along with the Abbott brothers. Two of the masked men quickly dismounted, and then they disarmed the Abbots. Lyle grumbled to Dirk, but then swung down at the leader's directions.

"Give us the key," the leader on horseback demanded.

"You ain't going to rob us?" Dirk asked in disbelief.

"Shut up, stupid," Lyle ordered as he dug out the key. He handed it to the person on foot who came to take it while the others kept rifles leveled at the pair. "Here."

The masked figure on foot, gun drawn, backed over in a familiar way to Slocum. He had a hard time suppressing a grin as Jen started to undo cuffs. There was no mistaking her steps.

"Now take off your boots," the leader ordered.

"Damn, you can't steal our boots!" Dirk whined.

Slocum watched as Jen unlocked his hands. Another dismounted member of the band brought over Lyle's gunbelt for him. Amused, Slocum listened to the bellyaching of the Abbot brothers as they sat on the ground and took off their boots. He strapped the gunbelt on his waist.

Later he would need a new hole for the buckle. The belt was too big, but for the time being it would work.

Jen slipped one of their rifles into his boot, and then

brought over a saddlebag. From the heft it was obviously filled with ammunition.

"You better take the packhorse too," she whispered softly.

"Thanks." he said, low enough that the two Abbots, still grumbling about what was happening, couldn't hear him.

"You aren't welcome in the territory," the leader said to them. "Take a stage and get out when you walk back to town. You try to follow him and your fate will be worse than this one."

"Here," Jen said, giving Slocum the lead to the packhorse. Then, in a lower voice: "You better take the medicine wheel way out. Watch out for those horse raiders."

"I will." He swung up in the saddle, taking the lead from her.

"You ain't seen the last of us, Slocum!" Dirk shouted after him. "You can't hide forever."

"Have fun walking," he said, and touched the brim of his hat to the others. He swung his horse westward, looking at the towering dark outline of the Bighorns. He would be more careful this time. The two raiders would probably be gone by the time he reached the area of the ambush, but further on, maybe at this Hole-in-the-Wall place, he might run into them.

The masked riders were dispersing. He could see them taking different directions as the loud cursing of Lyle echoed in the canyon. Intent on making plenty of tracks, Slocum rose in the stirrups and set the horse to trotting uphill.

He was making his way by the starlight, and paused to led the horses breathe. His ear turned to listen. There was another horse coming up the mountain after him. Who was it? Nat? Nicky? Jen? No telling. The masked riders had not let his friends talk out loud for fear that the Abbots would recognize them. Good move and well planned. Best of all, he realized as he rubbed where the cuffs had been, he was free.

Who was coming up his back trail? He set the horses on again until he reached a flat and a grove of juniper. Behind the shield of the resin-smelling evergreens, he waited.

The rider came into view, and stood in the stirrups to try to detect which way he had taken.

"Hold it right there!" he ordered.

"Slocum, that you?" Imagene asked.

"What are you doing up here?" he demanded, riding in close.

"Damn, I got half the folks at roundup to get you free and that's all you can ask?"

"I warned you—" He cut his words and rode in, and they embraced, kissing and almost unseating both of them when their horses shifted.

"I'm going along," she said, looking down at her horn.

"It—"

"I don't want to hear another negative word."

"Suit yourself, but don't say I didn't warn you," he said, and rode over to catch his packhorse. She might regret ever thinking about coming with him. He looked to the snowcapped peaks. They needed to be well over them by dawn. Booting his horse on, he hurried for the divide high overhead.

22

They camped the next day at noon in the high country, drank some stale canteen water, and gnawed on peppery jerky from the Abbots' supplies. Both silent, they hunkered down on their boot heels. The cool mountain air held a deep chill. She had not complained, and their pace coming over the range had been tough. If the pair of brothers had taken a stage out of Buffalo, they might have gotten off at Kaycee, bought more horses and set off after Slocum and Imagene's tracks in a day.

Ahead were some rock surfaces that would slow them down. Regardless of pursuit, Slocum knew they were both so bleary-eyed they needed to sleep a few hours before moving on again.

"You ever been to this hole-in-the-wall?" he asked Imagene.

"No, I've always heard that rustlers stayed there."

"Guess we'll both find out," he said, removing the roll from her saddle.

"We're going there?"

"Yes, those horse raiders must either be there or have been through there." He unfurled the blankets on the ground and then looked at her. "There room in this bed-roll for two of us?"

"Sure," she said, smiling wickedly.

Snuggled together still in their clothing, they fell fast asleep in each others arms. Slocum awoke before sun-down, eased himself out and went to check on their back trail. On the shady side of the mountain, he studied the deep purple vastness. No sign of anyone. He listened and heard nothing but the magpies crying as he went back to camp.

"We need to ride some more?" Imagene asked, sit-ting up on the bedding.

"Yes, lower down we can fork off this main trail and find us a secluded place to camp while I scout this hole-in-the-wall."

"Remember, I'm going with you," she said.

"You don't trust me?"

"I trust you fine. I simply didn't come along to sit back in camp like some blanket-ass squaw is all." She busied herself pulling on her boots.

"Yes ma'am, let's saddle, pack and ride. We can make another ten miles before we need to quit. I don't like narrow trails by starlight, but we can ride over the crest and past where they ambushed me."

"Are there narrow trails?" she asked in a little voice.

"Probably. I've never been there before, but I'd guess there are to get off this much height."

"Let's do them in the daylight."

"Sure," he smiled at her.

"More jerky and water?"

"That's the menu, only we need to eat as we ride. There isn't much daylight left."

"Oh, yes sir."

Hell, he didn't have time for all the niceties that she had at home. Maybe a week or so of this and she'd see the error of her ways and go back. He wished she would for her own sake. Heavens, he had to admit it was kind of breathtaking to wake up with her in the same bedroll, even if they were both too tired to do anything about it.

When the moon finally came up, they were miles down the far side, and the gentle descent surprised him. Why, rustlers could easily drive a herd of cattle over the mountain. What if real thieves had been taking her beef over this way, the ones she blamed Nat and the others for stealing? It made sense. If *they* could ride it by star-light and the way wasn't all that bad, then a few cow thieves could herd a small bunch over the same.

"I've been thinking about your losses." He turned in the saddle to face her.

"Yes, go ahead."

"You ever think they were taking them out of the country by this route?"

"I always figured the small ranchers were rebranding them for their own use."

"We'll see," he said. He felt certain there were FXT cattle somewhere up ahead, and he intended to show her the real thieves.

Dawn came over the Bighorns wall behind them. First, spears of sunlight showed, then the shadows began to shorten. A vast broken country spread out beneath them in the morning light. Miles of badlands, canyons, and small ranges of mountains shone bloodred under the new sun. The vastness made him feel small. There were a million places to push cattle, especially stolen ones, until their blotched brands healed.

"Where is this place at?" she asked, riding up beside him.

"Damn good question," he said. "Somewhere out there."

"I've been thinking that someone could have pushed cattle in here."

He nodded, wordless. There was possibly more than stolen cattle there. If they hadn't left, then the men who killed the boy were there—the same ones that shot Dunny, and he owed them for that. The next thing for Slocum to do was find them.

They rode until afternoon when he found a good stream with fresh water. Riding down the course, he located a bottom rich in grass for the horse stock. Several cottonwoods offered shade and a pleasant place to camp near the gurgling stream. It would have been an idyllic place for the two of them under less stressful circumstances. Now, he needed to find a deer for camp meat. If shrouded with the pack tarp, it was cool enough at night for the meat to keep several days.

One gun shot would never be placed. Though it might put the outlaws to looking, he still dared risk it. Chances were good that the brothers would never hear it.

"I'm going after a deer," he said, started unloading the packhorse.

"We need to hobble the horses?" she asked.

"Yes. I'll keep mine to hunt with."

"Good. While you're gone, I'll look through all this stuff in the panniers and find some honest food. My teeth hurt from gnawing on that tough jerky." She touched her jaw and made a face at him.

He winked at her as he set the canvass pack down. It was plenty heavy. He hoped there was more than empty whiskey bottles in it. She undid the flap on the first pack while he went after the next one. His job complete, he waved at her and mounted.

"Hey, they do have some real food and coffee in here." Imagene looked up and smiled. "I'll have coffee and rice cooking when you get back."

"Good," Slocum said and set off on the bay horse going down toward the bottom.

Rifle in his hands, he expected to spook up a mule deer any minute. He had seen a few coming in, but hadn't been ready to shoot one. Then two bolted and started up the slope. A flock of magpies, which were surrounding something dead, spooked at the same time. Slocum reined up the horse, took aim and fired. The yearling deer dropped in a heap, the other bounded away on springlike legs over the crest.

Slocum swung the gelding around and looked at the carcass. Someone had slow-elked a heifer. Not anxious to mess with a decaying corpse, still he dismounted and took hold of a hind hoof to toss the animal over. The brand on her hide was obvious: Bar C, Nat's brand. So, even the small ranchers' stock was being driven over the divide. Slow-elked for the steaks and left to rot, they were a brazen bunch. Taking only the prime cuts from an animal was a wasteful trick considered underhanded. Still, who was going to check on a dead animal up here?

Slocum led his horse near the deer, tied him to a juniper bough and began the task of dressing the deer. Prepared to gut the carcass, he looked up as Imagene came running toward him on foot. First, she stood on her toes at some distance from the smelly heifer and studied the brand he had exposed.

"You were right, Slocum," she said.

"I expect to find FXT cattle here, too." He raised up, standing straddle-legged over the deer, the bloody knife in his hand.

"I can help," she offered.

"Good, take that leg and hold it up," he said, indicating a front one as he bent over to open the belly with his blade.

"I've been wrong, haven't I?"

"Maybe," he said, too busy with butchering to talk to her.

"You knew it didn't you?"

"I knew Nat Champion was no rustler," Slocum said, brushing the sweat from around his eyes with his sleeve. Then he went back to work; learning never was easy if one had his mind set in stone.

"You like liver?" he asked.

"Not raw."

"Me neither. Cooked, it ain't bad," he joked, continuing his work to gut the deer.

23

He made small cooking fires. Nothing carried like the pungent scent of wood smoke, and it would give them away faster than anything else. He wanted their presence in this land to be unknown. The chances of them being discovered in these desolate badlands were slim, except by pure blundering. There were no other horse tracks in the area, save the old ones made by the slow elkers who had tracked the heifer down to shoot her.

It was the act of someone unscrupulous to slow-elk an animal. Leaving that much waste went against the grain with him. It wasn't particularly wrong to eat another's beef, but it was to squander better than three fourths of it. Besides, that heifer had not taken a fancy and come over the Bighorns this far from her home range without being brought up here. She'd certainly been rustled.

He took some time to sweep away their prints with pine boughs when they rode out to search for signs of where the rustlers hid out. Each day they went in a different direction, hoping to discover a place where the outlaws had stayed. Then, in the jumbled country to the south, they found fresh hoofprints on a narrow pathway through a maze of house-sized boulders.

Further inside the narrow passage, he spotted where someone had dismounted. He stepped off his horse and studied the heel marks with the exposed nails in the dirt.

"You see anything?" she asked, leaning over her saddlehorn.

"Yes, the horse-chousers were here." He remounted his horse and studied the jumble of flush-faced rocks ahead. Then he booted the bay through the narrow crevice. In places they were forced to go single file, his knees barely clearing the walls. He twisted in the saddle to check on her, wishing she had stayed behind; they could be riding into a trap.

"What are we going to do if we find them?" she asked softly above the plod of their horses' hooves.

"Cover that when we find them."

"You beat all, Slocum," she said behind him.

"How is that?" he asked without turning.

"You're running from two bounty men that captured you once, and you're more worried about capturing some worthless rustlers than your own safety."

"I owe them for shooting my horse,"

"No, it's the side of you I guess I like the best."

"What's that?" He turned and frowned at her as they continued riding up the crevice.

"I'm not sure what to call it. Toughness, fairness, I guess."

He reined up his horse and quickly dismounted. With a wary head shake to silence her questions, he stepped back and gave her the reins.

"What is it?" she hissed.

"I heard a horse whinny."

"You did?"

"Stay here. I'm going ahead on foot and see—"

"Put your hands in the air!" someone ordered from above them.

In disgust, Slocum saw him standing on top of the rock over them with a rifle in his hands pointed at them. He wore bat-wing chaps and a wool coat. His black bearded face was unfamiliar, but Slocum knew when he heard him walk closer to edge of the rock that he was the one with the nail-exposed boot heels.

"My, my, you are a sweet looker," the man said to Imagene. "Don't you two get any notions. Drop those guns slow-like. I'll get one of you if you try anything. Gabbard! Gabbard, get up here! We've got us company."

"We're in a mess, aren't we?" she asked under her breath.

"We'll see," Slocum said softly. How many of them were there? He needed to know that before he tried anything.

"Step back," the rustler ordered with a wave of his muzzle from his lofty place.

"What the hell brings you up here?" Gabbard asked, coming on foot up the trail with his six-gun in his hand. A shorter burly man, he was out of breath when he reached Slocum and Imagene. "Bates! It's the guy on the sorrel horse!" he said, excited about his discovery.

"He don't learn, does he?" Bates said, coming around from behind the rock.

"You ain't too smart, mister. You two get off those horses," Gabbard said.

"I come to cut a deal with you," Slocum said as the burly man stared at Imagene with a fascination that irritated him.

"Well, ain't you a fine-looking filly." Gabbard ignored him, looking rudely at her.

"I don't know your business, mister, but when the others get here you're on your way to being hung," she said. The cold defiance in her voice rang like a bell.

"Ha!" Gabbard laughed, and reached for her.

Gun or no gun, Slocum twisted him around and knocked the man's Colt loose, sending it spinning, then struck him with a powerful blow. He saw her dive for her pistol on the ground; things weren't going the way he wanted. Gabbard struggled to his feet and, raging like a grizzly, charged him. He stepped aside to avoid the man's rush as she fired at the other rustler as he came into view on the trail.

Gabbard's bear hug still freight-trained him backwards. Slocum drove two punches to the man's temples, but neither staggered his growling adversary. He drove another fist to Gabbard's ear as they spilled on the ground. The last blow took part of the man's fury, and he released part of his hold. Slocum used the opportunity to slip free, and scrambled to his feet to square off. As they circled each other, he saw that Imagene had the drop on Bates.

"You don't want to get shot in the leg, get your hands up," she ordered Gabbard. She punctuated her order with a shot that sprayed sand at both Gabbard and Slocum.

The rustler wilted and slowly raised his hands. Slocum stepped in and took the knife from his belt.

"We aren't a bad team, are we?" she said smugly as he shoved Gabbard toward his partner.

"Not bad at all. Who hired you boys?" he asked, taking Bates's gun and knife.

Neither of the rustlers spoke. He stepped over and hugged her shoulder with his gun hand. She had lots of grit.

"These two might talk more on the end of a rope," Slocum said. "Keep your wits, girl. Get the horses, I'll march these two out of here. There maybe another rattler in this den.''

''I'll watch for it,'' she said, sounding pleased with the turn of the events.

''You two want to tell me who hired you to run off those horses?'' he asked, walking behind the two.

''We ain't talking,'' Gabbard said.

''Guess you know there was a boy killed in one of those stampedes.''

''We don't know what you're talking about,'' Gabbard grumbled.

Slocum spotted the low-walled cabin in the swale that opened up at the end of the boulder bed. The small structure looked snug, and the nearby corral was big enough to hold a large herd of horses or cattle. Must be a spring around somewhere. He tried to be as cautious as possible in case there were more of them. Someone had taken lots of pains to build such a structure for such a remote place. These two were slow elkers, not crafted cabin builders, and not smart enough to benefit from running off horses so people couldn't go to roundup. At the very best, they were small-time rustlers hired by someone to do their dirty work.

''Whose place is this?'' Slocum asked as they marched across the open ground.

''It's—'' Bates was cut off by his partner's curt words.

''Don't tell him a damn thing!'' Gabbard snarled. ''Let him figure it out.''

He used the Abbott brothers' cuffs to hook the two together, and then chained them to a corral post. There were three outfits inside the cabin. He figured the extra bedding belonged to the dead breed.

She stoked the cabin's stove in good humor. Acting pleased, she busied herself making coffee and some dough for apple turnovers.

"Those raiders had some dried apples in that pannier," she said when he returned from putting up the horses. "Are they going to stay out there?"

"Safe as can be. Unless they can chew through those chains."

"Who are they?"

"Hirelings. They had nothing to gain by scattering horses unless they were paid for it. They never stole any of them. I'd say they ran small bunches of cattle over here, blotched the brands, and then pushed them off on some crooked trader. Enough to keep you and the small ranchers mad at each other." He shook his head, still wondering who was their boss. "They're lazy, and I figure that heifer they butchered was a little wild and she got away from them before they could re-do her brand, so they shot her for her steaks."

"What do we do next?" she asked, straightening from putting her pastry in the oven.

"Take them back to Buffalo to answer for the boy's death."

"I'll take them back." She frowned, concerned. "You can't go back there. Those two brothers are liable to be back in Buffalo looking for you."

"The Abbot brothers aren't that smart. They hired some of the major's helpers to find me the last time."

"It's still too dangerous. I'll go get your friend Nat Champion to come and take them to the sheriff."

"I thought you said he was a rustler." He grinned smugly at her.

"Well, they stole his cattle too." She hugged him and buried her face in his chest. "Maybe I was wrong about Nat. Have you forgiven me for trying to kill you?"

"I guess I have to."

"Are those two chained up good enough?" She looked up, shoving her hard breasts into his chest.

He acted like he was considering the matter, savoring

her closeness. Her grey eyes pleaded with him. Finally he grinned to break the impass, hugged her tight, then put his cheek on top of her head.

"They aren't going anywhere," he promised her.

"Good," she said, and leaned back to begin unbuttoning his shirt.

"What about your turnovers?"

"We can—no." She ducked out from under his arms. "I'll take the damn things out of the oven so they don't burn. I may forget them." She bent over and retrieved the pan.

He studied her shapely backside and drew a deep breath to settle himself inside. His plan to look for some of the re-branded cattle was about to be put off. Who cared? He closed his eyes as she returned—who the hell gave a damn anyway. As for the two rustlers chained up outside, it sure wouldn't make any difference to them.

24

Slocum stood in the doorway, faced the cool light breeze, and studied the gray dawn. Both prisoners were asleep under their blankets, still chained to the corral. The day before, he had found over fifty head of re-branded cattle. Several bore the FXT brand, changed to 88Z or 88T. Nat's Bar C had been changed to an H0. There were several other blotched changes on the cattle he had located in an easy circuit of the cabin.

The two rustlers had not answered a question he had asked. Imagene had become so angry with their sullen ways that she'd threatened to beat them with a lariat until they told the entire story. He'd had to bear-hug her and physically take her back to the cabin until her rage cooled. Besides, she made fierce love whenever she was mad—a good diversion.

This day they would take the prisoners back. When they reached the basin, they planned for her to go ahead and locate Nat. Slocum intended to turn them over to his friend someplace short of Buffalo, and let Nat take them to the authorities. He drew a deep sigh. After that he somehow had to convince her to stay behind, a river he'd have to ford before many more dawns. He glanced over as she slipped out of the covers. The shadowy light washed over her nakedness as he came across the cabin toward him.

Her short shapely legs took slow deliberate steps. She swept the long black hair back with both hands, her tea-cup breasts pointing upward. A devilish smile set on her lips as she drew closer.

"Let's stay here forever?" she asked in a husky voice, and then hugged him.

"I'd like to," he said. "But we both have lives. You have a ranch to run and I need to move on."

"Damn, damn, Slocum, it isn't fair." She buried her face in his vest.

"No one said it was going to be." He hugged her, rubbing her bare back as she held him tight.

"We need to leave today, don't we?"

"Yes."

"I'll fix us some food," she said in surrender.

"Good," he said, drawing in his breath for some control. She slipped away from him and went for her clothes. He watched her slowly dress. A big rock formed in the pit of his stomach; nothing was ever fair. It hadn't been for a long time in his life.

The ride over the top went uneventfully. Neither rustler said much. Gabbard complained some, and shut off anything Bates started to say. If the pair was separated, Slocum figured that Bates might talk. He'd tell Nat about that. The plan was to head for Buck's cabin. They could hole up there while she went for Nat.

It was past sundown when they reached the place. He locked the two up to a corral post, gave them jerky and a drink of water, and dumped their bedrolls off to them. Then he hobbled the horse stock. She had the lamp on in the cabin, and was no doubt stoking the stove, for he caught the scent of wood smoke as he finished with the stock. He went inside.

"Last of the deer," she said, standing over her cooking.

"Lasted long enough," he said.

She didn't look at him, only nodded and stared down at the sizzling meat.

"Hey, the camp!" someone shouted.

Slocum's hand went to his gun butt. He spotted his rifle on his saddle on the floor as she frowned at him.

"Get us loose!" Gabbard shouted. "There's a wild man out there!"

"Who the hell are you?"

"Don't get close to those two, Nicky!" Slocum shouted, hurriedly undoing the door as he recognized the young man's voice.

"That you, Slocum?"

"Yes, those are the horse-chasers," he said.

"I figured that you'd be three states away by now," the youth said, dropping off his horse.

"I got detained."

"Oh," he said, and blushed at the sight of her beside him in the lighted doorway. "Howdy, ma'am." He jerked off his hat.

"What are you doing up here?"

"I got confused riding these canyons, and was so far from camp by sundown I figured I could hole up here for the night and ride back in the morning."

"How's roundup going?"

"Well . . ." Nicky shook his head. "The major got over his illness, took over ramrodding the roundup, and he's been raising hell ever since. There's clear-cut cases of ownership of a calf and he overrules it. Him and Nat been nose-to-nose every day.''

"Maybe he needs another lesson.''

"I sure wish someone could figure out how.'' Nick dropped his head in hopelessness.

"You can't go—'' She cut off her words intended for Slocum, and then turned away. "Nicky, there's some food left. I'll fix you a plate.''

"Oh, yes, ma'am,''

They talked as he ate. Nicky was curious about the pair of rustlers outside. Slocum explained everything about their activities and what he suspected was their part in the deal. Finished eating, Nicky thanked her for the food and pushed his stool back from the table.

"I can take them to Buffalo for you,'' he said.

"I'll go along and help him,'' she offered, and turned to Slocum. "You can take your rig and head out.''

He nodded that he heard her, pleased it was her idea that they separate. The problem of the major still bothered him; someone needed to teach him a lesson. How could he help them? Maybe there was a way—there had to be something he could do about the overbearing man.

"Everyone will be headed into Buffalo tomorrow. It's Saturday night off,'' Nicky said offhandedly. "I bet a bunch of them get drunk after a week with that old bossy major.''

"Be interesting if we could get those two to talk,'' she said with a toss of her head.

"They will if they separate them,'' Slocum said.

"I'll tell the sheriff to do that,'' Nick said.

"Good, let's get some sleep,'' Slocum said, raising his hands over his head to stretch and yawn. It had been a long day.

"I'll bunk outside,'' Nicky said, acting uncomfortable.

"Plenty of room on the floor,'' Slocum said.

"Naw," Nicky said, and rose to his feet, obviously anxious to leave them alone.

Later in the bunk as she snuggled her warm subtle form against him, she softly mocked him. "Oh, sleep on the floor, Nicky."

"What would it hurt?" he asked.

"Plenty," she said, crawling up, dragging her breasts over his chest to raise up and kiss him. Her lips sealed off his further teasing.

At dawn, they separated. It was a quiet time. Slocum and Imagene stood close, and neither could find words.

"If I can ever help you. You need money for a lawyer. To get out of a fix." She chewed on her lower lip as she stood before him.

"Thanks, Gene. Be careful. You've stepped over a dangerous line in this ranching business. Choosing sides can be a necessity."

"I was wrong."

"There will be more problems ahead. Nothing's been solved, even if they get those two to talk." He tossed his head in their direction.

She woodenly nodded that she had heard him. Then he helped her mount up, and after he patted her on the leg, he went over and shook hands with Nicky.

"Take care of yourself, Slocum," the youth said.

"I will." He waved good-bye as they left with their prisoners.

Slocum took his time saddling his horse. He fidgeted with the pack animal and loaded him. There was little that he wanted to do, and somehow he couldn't get himself motivated to leave. There was nothing he couldn't think of short of killing the major to change the man. Even slippery elm bark tea hadn't worked. How many bottles of expensive whiskey had the man thrown away?

Finally mounted up, Slocum looked downrange toward Buffalo. Nothing he could do there. He started to turn his horse toward the mountains. No, he had to do something, one final try to help his friends. He stepped off and then unpacked the horse, storing the supplies in the cabin. Hobbling it, he let the animal go off to graze.

He started down the valley, keeping to cover and off the trail. Twice he spotted a wagon headed to town on the road, and ducked into the junipers. When the sound of the iron rims and plodding horses was gone, he moved again. No rush. He didn't want to reach Buffalo before dark anyway. Then he could move about more obscurely and see what he could do about the major.

He had hunkered down a few miles from the village for hours waiting for sundown. Now the sun had set, and he rode in the back way and put his horse in Mrs. Hawkins's shed. No doubt man like the major stayed in a hotel room. Which one, and how would he ever get access? He came up the alley and listened through the board-thin walls at the back of each saloon, hoping to hear some voices, some giveaway. But nothing turned up at any of those places. He grew more concerned. Either the man wasn't drinking, or Slocum couldn't detect it.

A drunk staggered down the alley past him, grunted "Hello," then ambled on in an unsteady way. Slocum ignored him. Where was his man? He took a chance and crossed the street. Then, through the cafe windows, he saw the man as he sat at a table waiting for his meal. It couldn't be anyone else, not with the four-peak hat, the broad chest encased in an army-like jacket, and the walrus mustache. Slocum dropped back in the shadows between the two buildings, sat down on his haunches, and began to whittle. He had all night.

"Been a tough week, Major?" someone asked when the big man came out of the cafe.

"They all are tough." With that he stomped off down the boardwalk. Slocum took up behind him. He remained twenty feet back until the man stopped to light a cigar. Then he hurried up directly behind him.

"Step in the alley," he said under his breath.

"I beg your pardon?"

"I don't have time for small talk. Step in the alley," Slocum said.

"You better have a good reason for this." The man obeyed, whipping out his match. "Who the devil are you?"

"That's not important. You know that doctored whiskey?"

"Yes. Are you the one?" He blinked at Slocum.

"Are you going to think every time you open a bottle of good whiskey for the rest of your life that it's been spiked?"

"What was in it?"

"Shut up and listen. If you don't want a rattlesnake in your bedroll or a cut cinch to pile your ass on the ground, you better start being reasonable to those small ranchers."

"That damn Champion sent you!"

"No one sent me. And you won't know when I strike again, but unless you got eyes in the back of your head, you better heed my words."

"I ought to beat the hell out of you for threatening me like this."

"Major, it wouldn't do you any good. See, you don't know how many more there are of us."

"Blackmail, and I'll not be threatened by trash like you!"

"Them two down at the jail sing, you may be in more trouble than with the roundup crew."

"What are you talking about?" the major demanded.

"Those two rustlers you hired to scatter horses."

"You're crazy. Mad. I never hired anyone—"

"That's not what they're saying."

"Liars hired by the damn rustlers themselves," he protested.

"Major, come Monday, if you aren't more accommodating to the other outfits during roundup, you better shake your bedroll and boots out every time you put them on. Watch your cinch too, it might be worn, and then check your saddle blankets for sand burrs."

"Just who in the hell are you?"

"That's not important. I've been in the military and I know what can be done to overbearing officers in the field."

"Look here!"

"No, I won't be looking. You're the one that'll be looking all the time. Be a damn shame if you fell off your horse and couldn't go to Washington because of injuries, wouldn't it."

"I've heard enough. Blast you! I'll not be made to crawl by any sniveling rustler!"

"Suit yourself, but if things come true, don't say I didn't warn you."

"I'll see you in Hell, man!" He pointed a finger accusingly at Slocum.

"Make sure they got a good fire going, because you will be there before I will. And look over your shoulder every once in a while, I might be there."

"You no good—" The man went for his gun butt.

Before he could draw, Slocum had his own gun in his fist and shoved the muzzle hard into the man's stomach. Enough was enough. Slocum had grown tired of their little game. Even a tough nut like Wolcott would take some heed.

"That's all, Major. You've had your chance and warning." Slocum jerked the man's .44 out of his holster and then put his own back. Deliberately, he ejected each shell out on the ground, meeting the big man's glare.

"Just remember, I'll be watching for you and what you do."

"You're a dead man, that's what you are," the major said through his teeth.

"Fine," Slocum said, and replaced the man's pistol with a hard shove that brought them face to face. "You better get to walking before I plug holes in your belly."

"I'll find you and when I do, mister, I'll make you rue this night."

"Watch for those snakes," Slocum said, and stepped back in the alley's darkness. "Follow me, you're a dead man, Major."

"I'll get you, damnit!" the man screamed after him, but he stayed put, and when Slocum rounded the corner of the building he could hear the major shouting for the law.

A grin on his face, he hurried for Mrs. Hawkins's shed. In the darkness, he slipped inside the dark barn and untied his horse.

"Slocum, that you?" a woman's voice asked.

"Yes." He recovered from the shock of discovery, weak-kneed as he regained his composure.

"What are you doing back here?" Jen hissed.

"I think I fixed the major for the rest of roundup," he said, and went on to explain how if a snakeskin was put in the man's bedroll, a few burrs put near his saddle pads, and maybe a cinch cut, it might change his way of carrying out the roundup.

"Great, but she went looking for you."

"She?"

"Yes, Imagene. Said she figured you'd hole up a day or so in the wall. Something like that." Jen shook her head. "And I want to thank you. Sandy Crocker doesn't seem to mind a tomboy. You were right."

"Good for you. I'll catch up with her. Tell Nat to get those things done. It was the best I could do short of killing the old man."

"You did wonderful. Ride easy, cowboy."

"Have those two rustlers talked yet?"

"No, but the Social Club has sent a high-priced lawyer up here to get them out on bond."

"How long has Gene been gone?" He tightened his cinch.

"A half day. And thanks," she said, gathering him in her arms. "If you don't mind kissing a tomboy goodbye."

"Heavens, no." And he kissed her hard and long—the cowgirl with the neatest rocking walk he'd ever see.

"You done good, Slocum," she said quietly as they slowly separated.

"Keep after that lawyer, you'll get him," he said, and swung on his horse. He had miles to cover.

It was midday when he came out of the narrow trail at the Hole-in-the-Wall leading the packhorse. Her horse nickered from the corral as he looked toward the house. She appeared in the doorway.

"Damn, Slocum, where have you been?"

"Getting enough grub and supplies to stay up here a while. How does that sound?" he asked as he dismounted and she raced to hug him.

"Good," she said, and buried her face in his vest. "I know it isn't forever, but I'll take a small slice of the cake."

"That's what we'll have," he said, and rocked her in his arms. "A small slice." Then he'd have to be heading on. Damn, it would sure be nice until then.

Epilogue

A few years later, Etta Watson took up a homestead in the Sweet Water Range. Nearby, Jim Averel also struck a land claim upon which he built a store and post office. Averel was an avid writer of letters to the editor criticizing the large ranchers in the territory.

One morning in July 1889, a wealthy, arrogant rancher Albert Bothwell, whose grazing holdings extended around their properties, along with his hired men, lynched both Etta and Averel side by side. Then to cover up their murderous deed, Bothwell began to put out lies about the pair. Etta was the supposed "Cattle Kate," the rustler queen, and it was told that way in the *Police Gazette*. Reportedly she was using her skills as a prostitute to receive stolen cattle, a charge disputed by the smaller ranchers, who were up in arms over their murders. As folks who knew her said, Etta actually was only trying to fulfill her lifelong dream to become a rancher. Jim Averel, as far as anyone knew, never owned any stock, but was rather a merchant with an urge to write strong letters of protest.

Unrest continued as two other small ranchers in the region were drygulched by parties unknown, despite strong suspicions that the blame lay at the door of the Cheyenne Social Club.

In the spring of 1891, a wild plot was concocted in those halls to hire a hundred gun toughs, and a death list was drawn up of all the small ranchers they wanted killed. This was to be the final step to eliminate the small ranchers in the region. It began in early April 1891. After a fast train ride to Casper, under the leadership of Major Frank Wolcott, an army of a hundred Texans debarked and set out on horseback up the front of the Bighorns to rid Wyoming of small ranchers once and for all.

At sunup, they managed to find Nat Champion and his cowboy, Nick Ray, at home. Both of them were on the kill list. The Texas Kid gunned down Nick and the war began. Nat was wounded dragging Nick's body inside, but he managed to single-handedly hold the army off all day, despite their setting the house on fire. He left a very dramatic diary before he was forced by the smoke to try to escape the structure and was gunned down by four bullets. Nat's valiant efforts gave the other Johnson County ranchers time to arm and meet the force head on. Only the intercession of President Benjamin Harrison and his sending of federal troops saved the major and his troops from annihilation.

The case against the invaders was moved conveniently to Cheyenne. Finally, only the murder charges for the deaths of Nick Ray and Nat Champion were left as the high-powered lawyers of the Cheyenne Social Club worked every angle to free the lot of them.

Slocum was in Soccorro, New Mexico, when he read the month-old newspaper.

Cheyenne, Wyoming.

Final charges against the defendants in the Wyoming Range War were dropped today by the state prosecutors. The Texas Kid as well as three other unnamed acomplices were released from custody today in the now-famous slaying of the Johnson County rancher Nat Champion and his hired man, Nick Ray, during the so-called "Texas Army Invasion" of the Buffalo area.

The reason for their release cited by the prosecutor was that the two witnesses staying at the Champion ranch at the time of the attack have disappeared and thus there is no testimony against the accused. A rumor in the region suggested that the pair sought for their account were bought off and quietly ushered from the territory. So closes the final chapter of terror and high-handed dealings by the giants of the livestock industry.

Slocum closed the paper and considered finding a dozen rattlesnakes and filling Major Wolcott's bed with them. Shaking his head in disgust, he went outside, mounted up, and rode west. He had pressing business in Globe, Arizona.

As for Imagene Furston, she never married, and operated the FXT Ranch until her death at age ninety-two. Her estate was dispersed by John Crocker, attorney-at-law, the son of Jenny and Sandy Crocker, a prominent lawyer also, and a Wyoming rancher. The Crockers were well known, as was Miss Furston, for siding with the smaller ranchers through all the strife in the territory and later during statehood.

JAKE LOGAN

TODAY'S HOTTEST ACTION WESTERN!

__SLOCUM AND THE LADY 'NINERS #194	0-425-14684-7/$3.99
__SLOCUM AND THE PIRATES #196	0-515-11633-5/$3.99
__SLOCUM #197: THE SILVER STALLION	0-515-11654-8/$3.99
__SLOCUM AND THE SPOTTED HORSE #198	0-515-11679-3/$3.99
__SLOCUM AT DOG LEG CREEK #199	0-515-11701-3/$3.99
__SLOCUM'S SILVER #200	0-515-11729-3/$3.99
__SLOCUM #201: THE RENEGADE TRAIL	0-515-11739-0/$4.50
__SLOCUM AND THE DIRTY GAME #202	0-515-11764-1/$4.50
__SLOCUM AND THE BEAR LAKE MONSTER #204	0-515-11806-0/$4.50
__SLOCUM AND THE APACHE RANSOM #209	0-515-11894-X/$4.99
__SLOCUM'S GRUBSTAKE (GIANT)	0-515-11955-5/$5.50
__SLOCUM AND THE GREAT SOUTHERN	0-515-11983-0/$4.99
HUNT #213	
__SLOCUM #214: THE ARIZONA STRIP WAR	0-515-11997-0/$4.99
__SLOCUM AT DEAD DOG #215	0-515-12015-4/$4.99
__SLOCUM AND THE TOWN BOSS #216	0-515-12030-8/$4.99
__SLOCUM AND THE LADY IN BLUE #217	0-515-12049-9/$4.99
__SLOCUM AND THE POWDER RIVER	
GAMBLE #218	0-515-12070-7/$4.99
__ SLOCUM AND THE COLORADO	
RIVERBOAT #219 (6/97)	0-515-12081-2/$4.99

Payable in U.S. funds. No cash accepted. Postage & handling: $1.75 for one book, 75¢ for each additional. Maximum postage $5.50. Prices, postage and handling charges may change without notice. Visa, Amex, MasterCard call 1-800-788-6262, ext. 1, or fax 1-201-933-2316; refer to ad #202d

Or, check above books   Bill my: ☐ Visa ☐ MasterCard ☐ Amex _____ (expires)
and send this order form to:
The Berkley Publishing Group   Card#_____
P.O. Box 12289, Dept. B   ($10 minimum)
Newark, NJ 07101-5289   Daytime Phone #_____
Signature_____
Please allow 4-6 weeks for delivery.   Or enclosed is my: ☐ check ☐ money order
Foreign and Canadian delivery 8-12 weeks.

Ship to:

Name_____	Book Total	$_____
Address_____	Applicable Sales Tax (NY, NJ, PA, CA, GST Can.)	$_____
City_____	Postage & Handling	$_____
State/ZIP_____	Total Amount Due	$_____

Bill to: Name_____

Address_____City_____
State/ZIP_____

First in an all-new series from the creators of Longarm!

BUSHWHACKERS

They were the most brutal gang of cutthroats ever
assembled. And during the Civil War, they sought justice
outside of the law—paying back every Yankee raid with one
of their own. They rode hard, shot straight, and had their
way with every willin' woman west of the Mississippi. No
man could stop them. No woman could resist them. And no
Yankee stood a chance of living when Quantrill's Raiders
rode into town...

Win and Joe Coulter become the two most wanted men in
the West. And they learn just how sweet—and deadly—
revenge could be...

Coming in July 1997
BUSHWHACKERS by B. J. Lanagan
0-515-12102-9/$5.99
Look for the second book in September 1997
BUSHWHACKERS #2: REBEL COUNTY
also by B. J. Lanagan 0-515-12142-8/$4.99

VISIT THE PUTNAM BERKLEY BOOKSTORE CAFÉ ON THE INTERNET:
http://www.berkley.com

Payable in U.S. funds. No cash accepted. Postage & handling: $1.75 for one book, 75¢ for each
additional. Maximum postage $5.50. Prices, postage and handling charges may change without
notice. Visa, Amex, MasterCard call 1-800-788-6262, ext. 1, or fax 1-201-933-2316; refer to ad #705

Or, check above books	Bill my: ☐ Visa ☐ MasterCard ☐ Amex _____ (expires)
and send this order form to:	
The Berkley Publishing Group	Card# _____
P.O. Box 12289, Dept. B	Daytime Phone # _____ ($10 minimum)
Newark, NJ 07101-5289	Signature _____

Please allow 4-6 weeks for delivery.   **Or enclosed is my:** ☐ check ☐ money order
Foreign and Canadian delivery 8-12 weeks.

Ship to:

Name_____	Book Total	$_____
Address_____	Applicable Sales Tax	$_____
	(NY, NJ, PA, CA, GST Can.)	
City_____	Postage & Handling	$_____
State/ZIP_____	Total Amount Due	$_____

Bill to: Name_____

Address_____City_____
State/ZIP_____

A special offer for people who enjoy reading the
best Westerns published today.

If you enjoyed this book, subscribe now and get...

TWO FREE WESTERNS

A $7.00 VALUE—NO OBLIGATION

If you would like to read more of the very best, most exciting, adventurous, action-packed Westerns being published today, you'll want to subscribe to True Value's Western Home Subscription Service.

TWO FREE BOOKS
When you subscribe, we'll send you your first month's shipment of the newest and best 6 Westerns for you to preview. With your first shipment, two of these books will be yours as our introductory gift to you absolutely *FREE* (a $7.00 value), regardless of what you decide to do.

Special Subscriber Savings
When you become a True Value subscriber you'll save money several ways. First, all regular monthly selections will be billed at the low subscriber price of just $2.75 each. That's at least a savings of $4.50 each month below the publishers price. Second, there is never any shipping, handling or other hidden charges— *Free home delivery.* What's more there is no minimum number of books you must buy, you may return any selection for full credit and you can cancel your subscription at any time. A TRUE VALUE!

Mail the coupon below
To start your subscription and receive 2 FREE WESTERNS, fill out the coupon below and mail it today. We'll send your first shipment which includes 2 FREE BOOKS as soon as we receive it.

- -

Mail To: **True Value Home Subscription Services, Inc. P.O. Box 5235
120 Brighton Road, Clifton, New Jersey 07015-5235**

YES! I want to start reviewing the very best Westerns being published today. Send me my first shipment of 6 Westerns for me to preview FREE for 10 days. If I decide to keep them, I'll pay for just 4 of the books at the low subscriber price of $2.75 each; a total $11.00 (a $21.00 value). Then each month I'll receive the 6 newest and best Westerns to preview Free for 10 days. If I'm not satisfied I may return them within 10 days and owe nothing. Otherwise I'll be billed at the special low subscriber rate of $2.75 each; a total of $16.50 (at least a $21.00 value) and save $4.50 off the publishers price. There are never any shipping, handling or other hidden charges. I understand I am under no obligation to purchase any number of books and I can cancel my subscription at any time, no questions asked. In any case the 2 FREE books are mine to keep.

Name _____

Street Address _____ Apt. No. _____

City _____ State _____ Zip Code _____

Telephone _____ Signature _____

Terms and prices subject to change. Orders subject to acceptance by True Value Home Subscription Services, Inc.

(if under 18 parent or guardian must sign)

12070-7